A FLASH OF LIGHTNING, AN EARTHSHAKING CRASH—

And then the lights went off. The room was pitch, a big threatening cauldron of tar in which Julie stood almost afraid to breathe.

Suddenly there was a sound in the hall. She watched the door, hypnotized. The noise came on.

It was the sound of someone walking slowly toward her in bedroom slippers. Sssh-flap, sssh-flop, on it came. Julie felt suddenly and completely terrified, and all her scorn of ghosts and such myths evaporated. She began to imagine what it looked like. A squeak of horror escaped from her.

The noise stopped, and then began again, like weird smashing footsteps up and down the hall. While she might not believe in ghosts, Julie knew she was afraid. . . .

SIGNET Young Adult Titles by the Same Author

BONNIE
and the
Haunted Far

by
Barbara Van Tuyl

A SIGNET BOOK
NEW AMERICAN LIBRARY
TIMES MIRROR

SIGNET TRADEMARK REG. U.S. PAT. OFF. AND FOREIGN COUNTRIES
REGISTERED TRADEMARK—MARCA REGISTRADA
HECHO EN CHICAGO, U.S.A.

SIGNET, SIGNET CLASSICS, MENTOR, PLUME AND MERIDIAN BOOKS
are published by The New American Library, Inc.,
1301 Avenue of the Americas, New York, New York 10019

FIRST PRINTING, OCTOBER, 1974

5 6 7 8 9

PRINTED IN THE UNITED STATES OF AMERICA

This book is for Margaret Teller Riggs—

*a very special person
and a very special friend.*

Chapter 1

At 11:27 of a crisp and beautiful morning, Julie Jefferson was running toward the brood-mare barn. This was not unusual, for Julie had never believed in walking when she could run. Life was full of so many things to do. . . .

Clutched in one hand was an assortment of envelopes, magazines, and advertising fliers, while the other was stretched above her head waving a pamphlet at whoever might be watching her. As she neared the barn, Julie began calling, "Leon! Leon? Where are you?" When silence answered her, she altered course in midstride and headed away from the big front doors, tearing along toward the back of the barn and the mare fields.

"Leon!"

Rounding the far corner, she found him. With headlong force, a blonde-haired projectile, she slammed into him and sent them both sprawling amid papers and envelopes. Leon said *Oof* and Julie said *Wow* and they disentangled themselves. "Something wrong?" was all Leon could manage as he rolled over and groped for his glasses and hat in the tall grass. "Horse in trouble at the main barn?" His hand closed on the spectacles and he wheezed relief; they were brand-new, his first pair, and he had fought the idea of them for years, but now prized them greatly. He adjusted them carefully on his nose, retrieved his hat, and focused on the girl. "What's funny?"

"I don't know. Us. Me. It's mid-January and a simply gorgeous spring day. And your poor hat's squashed because I sat on it—"

"Ho ho," said Leon Pitt heavily. He suppressed a chuckle himself. The girl's good spirits were infectious. "I agree

7

with you about the day. But when you find humor in an aged black gentleman being turned upside down before lunch, we part company."

"You know I wouldn't laugh if you were hurt!"

"I know it. What's that you're grippin' like a crawdad with a nibble of hamburger? Top secret at least, to be worth all this commotion."

"I was coming to show you. It's a prize list for the Cochranville horse show. *You* remember—I said it was coming up soon. Lisa's sent it to me with her classes marked and a note asking us to come over and watch her and the filly. It'll be her first time out and—"

"The filly," said Leon, dusting his hat on his leg. "The filly?"

"Lights Out! The gray filly that we broke for her two years ago. She'll be just coming four now, and I guess this'll be her very first show."

"I can't seem to place the lady, but no doubt it will come to me after some thought."

"You never forgot a horse in your life."

"Wait now," said Leon quizzically. "The gray that nobody could get a bridle on. It took even the mighty Pitt two weeks to do it," he nodded.

"I always meant to ask how you finally did get the bit in her mouth, much less the rest of it over her ears. I was at the track with Bonnie when you did it."

"I resorted to the old wintergreen Life Saver trick. Candy's a fine training aid with horses, you know, when everything else fails."

"Well, anyway, would you like to go? Do you think we could? Maybe Monty'd come with us. No, even if he were home for it," said Julie, "I don't suppose he'd be too anxious to go to a horse show. Well, Lisa didn't mention him, just you and me. So will we go?"

Leon laughed. He was used to her continual enthusiasm about anything concerning horses. "Wait a tick. I don't even know when it is. I suppose it tells you, somewhere on that prize list?"

"Scheduled for next Saturday, and begins at 9:00 A.M. Lisa's first class isn't till 11:30, so if I could get done up a little early, we'd have time to catch it. Can we go? I'd sure like to."

"If there's one thing I've learned in all these years I've spent with horses, it's what I've tried hardest to din into you: the only predictable thing about 'em is their unpredictability. But if one of the mares in yonder doesn't decide to foal in the small hours of Saturday morning, or have a bellyache, or forget how to eat, and no other crisis pops up before we leave, I think it'd be good to take leave and go over for a while. I might even run into a couple of people I know," said Leon, shaping his old hat and setting it carefully on the top of his head. "As the uncrowned king of Fieldstone Farm, I say we'll go."

"Your uncrown has some dust on it," said Julie, squinting up at him. "Mary Anne will skin you. Oh, you dear Leon Pitt!" She hugged him. "Hey, do you think Nana would like to go? She's never been to a horse show. And beagles are notoriously fine horse-show dogs, and—"

He rolled his dark eyes upward, a smile of disbelief creasing his face. "Julie, Julie. Nana doesn't need to go to a horse show. You know perfectly well that you can't bear to keep her leashed, and before we knew it she'd be over at the food stand begging, or snootin' into some poor soul's lunch. Or she'd take off a-hunting. Or worse yet, she'd start moving people's brushes and sponges and tack, and everything else that didn't bite her first. Her middle name is Incorrigible."

Julie laughed. "And you'll remember that her last name is Pitt." Leon had given her the pup a little less than a year before. "You're right. My beagle would get into trouble, but I really don't know why! She always looks so responsible!" She gathered up the scattered mail. "Here, Leon, would you put the paper on the lunch table? You'll get there before I do, and somebody'll want to look at it. I'm going to run this stuff up to the big house. Oops, here's one for you. See, I came right from the mail box—"

"So I gathered. I'll take the paper, but first I want to take one more look around for Bandicoot's halter. I was out in the top field hunting it when I heard you bawling for me. Now that I see no crisis is afoot . . ."

"Well, I was excited," said Julie.

"Right. See you later, honey."

Later was quite a time off, for when Julie returned to her cottage to let her dogs out—she had adopted one of the stable St. Bernards some months before to keep Nana company—she was dismayed to find one small beagle lying contentedly in the middle of the living room, jaws wrapped securely around (and all sixty-eight teeth sunk deep into) Julie's favorite eiderdown quilt. Feathers blanketed the room in great gossamer snowdrifts.

"Oh, Nana! How *could* you?" she wailed. "My favorite, favorite quilt!"

The dog thumped her tail gaily.

"No use crying over spilt feathers," said Julie resignedly. "I'd punish you if I thought you'd have any notion what it was for. But you wouldn't." She scowled. "I'd have sworn I left you locked in the kitchen. At least I would have almost sworn it. It's more than obvious that I didn't. Must have forgotten." She looked at the other occupant of the room.

"And Pushy! You of all people! How could you let her do it?" The drowsing St. Bernard lifted his head at the sound of his name and gazed mournfully into her face over a pair of neatly folded forepaws.

"I know, it's not your fault. I can't hold you responsible for the errors of Nana, but couldn't you even try to talk her out of some of these capers? You're such a gentleman, and she's such a terror. Well," said Julie, "out you both go for a few minutes, while I attack this mess." Out they padded, and she set to work.

Feathers are as hard to collect as spilled mercury. When she finally appeared for lunch, everyone had eaten and gone except for Leon Pitt, Fieldstone foreman and Julie's mentor. "Hi," she said. "You wouldn't believe what Nana's done this time—shredded my marvelous old eiderdown quilt. And the funny thing is that the more I think about it, the surer I am that I left her locked in the kitchen this morning, just to avoid such a calamity. The only other person in the house was Pushy, and of course he won't say a word on the matter. And now Nana's gone hunting because I raised my voice to her."

"Nana's mother," said Leon, counting on his fingers, "went through quite an assortment of edibles in her younger days: six slippers, three galoshes, one blanket, two pillows, four chair legs, numerous bridles and halters and part of a saddle; and that's a partial list. Nana comes by her chewing honestly. Can't say the same for her Houdini trick. You must have forgotten to latch the kitchen door."

"This one's a knob. A latch I could understand, by accident, but—hey, Leon, what's this?"

He grinned. "Last I heard it was called a 'newspaper,' and it's delivered here at the farm three hundred and sixty-five days a year. What's what?"

"Silly. This photograph of the spooky-looking place."

"I didn't get that far today, Julie. Got hung up on the sports pages myself. Nat was looking at that section. Let's see." He scanned the article. Then he said thoughtfully, "Notice of public auction. The old Croydon farm's up for sale, according to this; lists the assets and the property to be sold . . ."

"Croydon Farm," repeated Julie. "I thought it looked familiar. It's that kind of rundown place off Route 143 just outside Meriden, isn't it? Why would anyone want to buy a hovel like that?"

"*That* used to be a lovely, working farm at one time, honey; way back in *my* time. It's fallen into disrepair—into *despair* might be a better way to say it—but there's quite a bit of land to it, and if somebody's willing to put time, money, and tender lovin' care into it, it could be fixed up really nice again."

"How old is it, Leon?"

"Let's see." He furrowed his brow, always careful that his answers should be accurate. "It was built around the time Stateside and Wish Me Well were running good, so that'd be in the middle thirties. Actually, the original farmhouse was put up before World War I but it burned, and wasn't rebuilt till the Croydons bought the place during the Depression."

"It says sealed bids. Maybe if I offered—"

"You don't need any part of the Croydon place, Julie Jefferson, so you can put that notion right outside your head," he said with unusual sternness.

"I was only kidding. But I really do love old things. They always remind me of Dad's antique shop. And maybe the thirties weren't so long ago if you were living then, but it looks so . . . well . . . so ancient. As if they'd imported it from Ireland or someplace." An intense expression came over her pretty young face. "Meriden's right on the way to Cochranville. You think we might stop there on the way to the horse show, or maybe on the way home, and just take a little old look around?"

"I most certainly do not. Not going *to* a horse show, not coming *from* a horse show, not on an expedition to foreign parts, nowhere, no way. I want no part of Croydon Farm, and neither do you. That's that."

She stared at this vehemence. "But why? You said it used to be a beautiful spread. Why are you so down on it all of a sudden?"

"It was beautiful, Julie, but that was before." He shut his mouth tightly.

"Oh, for heaven's sake, Leon! Before what?"

"That old place is haunted," he declared.

"Haunted? By what?" she asked in disbelief. "*You* don't believe that any more than I do. I suppose the resident ghost is supposed to drag his chains behind him with his head under his arm shrieking curses and threats to anybody who dares set foot there? Or is it a she, in a long white gown, who walks in the moonlight braiding her pale hair—"

"You is jess a-funnin' with yo' pore old Uncle Tom, missy," said Leon. "I guess 'haunted' is the wrong word. Just say the place has a bad reputation—a sort of bad feel to it, and it's a fine place to keep away from."

"Leon, will you please quit talking in circles and explain whatever it is you're talking about?" she demanded.

"You're worse than Nana after a rabbit when your curiosity's up, you know that? It isn't a pretty story, but you won't give me any peace till it's told, so . . .

"Like I said, the Croydons came to that farm sometime in the thirties. They were a young couple then, and hadn't any children. Carter Croydon was a good man. Good farmer, good neighbor, well-thought-of in these parts. There wasn't a soul had a harsh word for him, or for Martha either. She was your real old farm wife. Did her share of the chores and still set a fine table, baking bread and cookies and listening to folks' troubles, all that kind of thing. I think most Americans used to be that way. Well." He sighed.

"After a while their son Christopher was born, and they were the happiest pair in the world. The farm was growing and they were gettin' on nicely. One day—little Chris was four, maybe five years old—Carter went to town, leaving Martha alone with the boy. Somehow Chris managed to slip away, and took himself up to the pond; it lay off in an unused corner of the farm. Of course he'd been cautioned never to go there alone, but you know little boys don't always do what you tell 'em. He must have taken it into his head to go fishing, or hunting tadpoles, or some other stunt little boys take a fancy to. Anyway, Julie, that little boy was drowned there."

"How terrible!" she gasped. "But you don't mean that Croydon's haunted by the ghost of a child?"

"No. There's more, and as bad or worse. In the years that crept along after Christopher's death, the Croydons tried to fill their lives with just the farm and each other. Believe me, it showed it. It became the richest farm in the valley. Their crops were the biggest, their cattle the fattest —never a fence line in disrepair or a mud wallow anywhere. It was the envy of farmers for miles around. But the Croydons themselves weren't envied, they were pitied. I used to feel sorry and sad for them just ridin' past, thinkin' on that tragedy. They were such *good* people.

"Anyway, the farm wasn't really enough for them, 'cause when the infant boy who belonged to a new couple in Meriden was orphaned in a car crash, the Croydons brought him home and raised him like their own. I suppose they legally adopted him, but I don't guess it would've mattered to their feelings if they had or hadn't."

Leon shook his head. "How they did love that kid! Gave him anything he wanted. Treated him better'n their own. By and large he was a good boy, only a little spoiled. Isn't good for anybody to get everything handed to him. Now if you'd been given that treatment, you know you wouldn't be the sweetest girl in Kentucky—"

"Go on with the story," said Julie, holding her breath.

"For Carl's seventeenth birthday, they gave him a sports car. I mean a real one, speed to spare, all the chrome extras and fancy big engine and all that. Bright red, it was, I remember, and I used to see him takin' these roads at seventy and more.

"He changed then. Started spending a lot of time in Carneyville, Lakeland, and towns further out. His friends weren't kids from the local families that he went to school with. They may have been all right, but we didn't know them, never saw much of them, and wondered if they were the right kind for a boy of the Croydons.

"Anyway, one night, seems he met one of those friends up in Lakeland. He was acting peculiar. Kind of *high* is what the papers said afterwards. So his friend made some comment about this unusual behavior, and Carl said something that made headlines all over the country. 'You're right I'm high! I just killed my folks.'"

Julie put her fingertips to her mouth, shocked horribly.

"Well, how that other young fellow ever kept his wits about him is beyond me. But somehow, he managed to talk Carl into surrendering to the police. The newspapers had it all. Carl argued with his buddy. Said nobody'd ever suspect him. But that boy had some sense. Just kept on talking quietly. Told him how it'd go easier with him if he gave himself up, and that above all he mustn't run. So finally that's what Carl did, went to the law.

"When the sheriff and his men got out to the farm, the Croydons were dead all right. Murdered while they were eating their Sunday supper in the study by the fireplace. It was a real tragedy. Everyone hereabouts was just stunned, but when they lived with it a day or two, feelings started running pretty high against Carl, who'd been treated so wonderfully by those fine people, and so they had to take the trial to another town. What with him still bein' a minor, and the murder weapon never found, I don't think he could have been executed anyway. But he was put down as insane and locked up in an asylum, and far's I know he's been there ever since. If he'd been released I'd have heard about it, even when I was retired down in North Carolina, 'cause I kept in touch with lots of friends."

He leaned back; he had been tense on the edge of his chair, and now he gave a small shudder and began to relax.

"So you see, Julie honey, the ghosts that walk at Croydon Farm have a right to seek out a murderer, and if I got my legends straight, they won't rest till he dies . . . or something like that. Maybe there aren't any ghosts, maybe there are. I wasn't ever one to say for certain that anything *can't* be true. But Croydon's an unhealthy location, and curiosity's a mighty poor excuse for a girl to go pokin' around there. You see what I mean?"

"Oh, yes, Leon. I didn't understand. I still don't believe in ghosts—but what a sad story. It makes me want to cry for those poor, kind people. And no, I don't want to see the place. Not ever."

"Very sensible," said Leon Pitt.

Chapter 2

Saturday dawned, as fine a winter morning as Kentucky ever showed, breezy and fair with that nip in the air that wakes you up and makes you want to move around and do things. Julie's feet hit the floor at the alarm's first murmur. She shoved her two sleepy dogs out the door, warning them not to stay long, and began to gather herself together for the morning's work. For once the beagle obeyed her orders, returning almost at once to the door and signaling with a timid scratch. Julie let her in and she made a beeline for the bed from which she'd been ousted and promptly was twitching in rabbit-chasing dreams.

Pushy also reappeared in his saintlike fashion and waited for his mistress to remember that he was outside. With a hug and a biscuit for each of them, Julie was gone, remembering that this was the day of the horse show and that she'd better hurry if she was going to be finished in time to attend it.

The lights were just coming on in the mare barn as she drew alongside and, leaving the engine running, jumped out and dashed inside. "Hi, Bonbon! How's my best big lady-in-waiting this morning?" she called to the great bay mare in the first stall. A throaty snuffle as she blinked the sleep from her eyes, then Sunbonnet, the handsomest piece of horseflesh that anyone ever had the pleasure of seeing, opened her mouth and answered Julie with a full-throated neigh. Spirited, courageous, with a stride to eat the furlongs and a heart full of love for Julie Jefferson, this was Bonnie: bought as a wreck of a filly out of a muddy river in a junkyard, nursed to health and championship, named Three-year-old Filly of the Year and Handicap Filly of the Year, she had shattered a sesamoid bone (behind her left fore-ankle) and been retired from the track little more than a year ago, and was now in foal to Scotch Tweed, a well-proven sire who also resided at Fieldstone Farm. Bonnie was just past her official fifth birthday and within a month of her time.

The girl hurried to her stall, pulling from her pockets a carrot and four large gumdrops. These were offered on an outstretched palm as she patted the mare's neck affectionately with the other. Bonnie inhaled the carrot and crunched it, then daintily lifted three of the candy bits and savored them.

Julie stared at her, moist palm still holding one gumdrop. "Morning, morning, morning," said Leon behind her, pushing up the large grain cart filled with oats and all the special additives that comprise the brood-mare diet.

"Hi, Leon. Is something wrong with Bonnie? She only ate three of her favorite treats. She isn't going to foal *today*, is she?"

"Nothing wrong that I know about, Julie. She's not due to foal for another four weeks. As if you didn't know that to the hour! Don't you fret, she'll be giving us plenty of warning."

"But this gumdrop," said Julie, gazing at it blankly.

"I'll bet it's green."

"How'd you know? What does that have to do with it?"

"Great guns, Julie, how'd you like to look at green gumdrops first thing in the morning on an empty stomach? Besides, she's never been partial to lime. Find something else to worry about."

"Well, as long as you're sure she's okay. . . . Did anything interesting happen around here last night?" This was delivered so pseudo-casually as to be genuinely funny, and Leon laughed.

"How do you mean that 'interesting'?"

"Oh, Leon, this is Saturday!"

"Saturday. Yes, I guess it is, yesterday bein' Friday, if an oldtimer's memory serves him."

She looked at Bonnie's placid face and counted to ten

by fives. "Leon, Saturday. You haven't really forgotten.
The day of the horse show!"

"Oh! You mean has anything happened around this
barn to prevent someone from going to a horse show,
that is, if someone else got done in time to go with
someone?"

"Will you be able to go?"

"Will you?"

"I'm on my way, honestly. I've only got three colts and
two fillies that I absolutely must get on this morning. If
they get a day off they seem to lose two days' progress.
But when I finish with them, I'll help the boys walk the
others, and we should be done by ten. That'll give me
half an hour to get cleaned up—I'm going! What about
you?"

"Way things look, we'll be off and running at your con-
venience."

"Super! Be back at quarter of eleven." Looking something like the tardy rabbit in *Alice,* she fled toward her
idling car. Bonnie whickered a farewell, and Leon glanced
up at her, startled. The horse really did talk to the girl.

"You're the least average racehorse I ever did know,"
he told the bay, "but you're the best too, and I guess the
two facts go hand in hand. You're all horse, but sometimes you're a little too human to accept easy."

The mare rolled an intelligent and affectionate brown
eye at her old friend, but said nothing further.

The Cochranville horse show was well under way when
they arrived. Horses groomed to the back teeth and riders
brave in their Sunday best were everywhere. Vans and
trailers, gaily hung with prize ribbons testifying to honors
already garnered by the occupants, were parked neatly
around the perimeter of the show grounds. Classes were
being held simultaneously in two rings and on the outside
course, while horses, ponies, children, and adults hustled
from one place to another in order to be on time and not
miss their turns in the order of jumping.

"Sort of like Barnum & Bailey in the good old tent days,"
said Leon reminiscently. "Three rings goin' strong and
the clowns up to their tricks on the hippodrome track—

man, you never knew what to look at first! But I was forgetting, Julie, you aren't old enough to have seen that. Maybe this is the nearest thing to it you'll ever know."

She was gazing round in amazement at the throng of humans and horses. "I didn't know there were ever this many horsey people anywhere except at the track," she said to Leon, who was searching for familiar faces in the crowd. "How do we find Lisa in this crush?"

"It's a little confusing at first, but like the circus, once you know your way around and where to look, it's no harder than locatin' someone on the backside at the track. All in knowing where to go. You said she'd be showing in the young hunter classes, right?"

"I think so." Julie rummaged in her purse for Lisa's note.

"Then we eliminate that ring over there," he pointed, "the one with no jumps in it. That'll be for the children's equitation and flat classes. They may be holding her classes on the course or in the other ring. We'll just have to check both places." They walked toward the outside course. Before they were near enough to discover what class was in progress, Leon was greeted warmly by a jovial man with a bulging middle section.

"Leon Pitt, what are you doing at a horse show? Did you bring anything?"

Leon grinned. "Gerry, this is Julie Jefferson. Julie, Gerry Jackson. We didn't bring any horses, no. Just came to see a filly we broke at Fieldstone a couple years back. Do you know what class is going on on the course or in the hunter ring now?"

"Miss Jefferson, charmed. I'm not sure, Leon," the big man said. "Because of a whopping lot of entries, they're running late; which means I'll be here half the evening— Jessica sure won't leave till the bitter end. I know they haven't had any young or green hunters go outside yet, just juniors and working so far. Come over to the van and see Jess and her new colt while I check the time schedule and figure out where we are."

They headed for his van. Gerry pointed at an attractive brown gelding coming toward them, led by a young woman. "Here she comes now. Must be getting ready for something."

"Will you give me a leg up, grandpa?" the woman asked Gerry. "They called the 'under saddle' ten minutes ago but I don't see anyone over there yet."

"D'you know what's on the course now?" her grandfather asked as he lifted her lightly into the saddle.

"Green, then young, then us again," she told him, and walked the gelding off for the flat ring as her class was called over the loudspeaker.

"That was Jessica," said Gerry. "She'd have loved to meet you if she could have seen anything but horses."

"This one," said Leon, thumbing at Julie, "is precisely the same. She only talks to me 'cause she thinks I'm an old war-horse."

"That's not true!" said Julie. "Well, yes it is, I guess." Her roaming gaze was caught by a girl who was lunging a gray horse—that is, making it move in a circle while held by a long rein—in a quiet corner out of the general commotion. "There's Lisa and Lights Out, I think," she told her friend hurriedly. "I'm going to make sure. Good luck to Jess in the under saddle, Mr. Jackson! I hope the colt wins." She was gone.

"Funny how it gets girls like those two, isn't it?" said Gerry. "Never anything but horses-horses-horses from breakfast to bedtime."

"How curiously unlike fellows such as you and me," said Leon.

"Just what I was going to say. Unfathomable!"

Lisa Marsden was delighted to see Julie, and anxious to hear at once how she thought the filly had progressed since leaving Fieldstone. Julie was honestly enthusiastic, and after the first young hunter class, in which Lights Out was pinned fourth, it was hard to say which of the two was more excited. Since it would be at least an hour and a half before the filly would go again, she was cleaned up and loaded on her trailer with a full hay net hung in front of her. Then the girls set out for the food stand for a soda and girl-talk.

"What are you doing now, Julie? It's been so long.

How's Bonnie? And Monty and Leon and everyone, and
that lovely jockey what's-his-name, Beau, and—"

Julie laughed. "A dose of my own medicine. Okay!
Bonnie's just fine, due to foal in less than a month, and
her leg's great. Monty's at Kandahar most of the time—"

"Has he asked you to marry him yet?"

"Marry him?" repeated Julie blankly. "He's never
asked me for a date!"

"The way he looks at you, I thought your whole lives
were one long date," said Lisa. "What are you blushing
about?"

"The sun's hot," said Julie. "Anyhow, Monty just pops
in and out of the farm now and then when he can, and I
hardly see him. We're *so* busy. . . . Leon's here at the
show somewhere, and I'm sure he saw your trip with
Lights Out. Everyone else is great. And you remember
me talking about Stash Watkins? The man at St. Clair
Farm who helped me raise Bonnie?"

"Beau's father?"

"Right. He's come to Fieldstone too. St. Clair went out
of the breeding business and only handles racing stock
now, and since the 'mommies and babies' are Stash's true
loves, he's come to work for Mr. T, just like Monty and
Beau and me."

"Are you still going to the track?" Lisa asked. "I wasn't
really sure you'd get my letter in time when I sent it to
the farm."

"I've hardly been to the track at all since Bonnie was
hurt. With her getting ready to foal, you can bet I won't
go far now, either. There's plenty for me to do at Fieldstone. We've started to break our two-year-olds, and I
get on about eight a day and when I'm finished with them
and I've cleaned my tack, it's usually around eleven. That
leaves me just barely time enough to spend with Bonnie
and the pups. Or come to a horse show."

"Or go to a movie with Monty?"

"He doesn't go to movies. He worries about racehorses."

"You ought to get yourself a horse to show, as much as
you love 'em and as good as you are with 'em," said Lisa.
"Better yet, make one. That's more than half the fun."

"I think it must be," agreed Julie. "Funny you should mention it. Looking at this place today, with all that's going on, I've sort of been toying with the idea that I'd enjoy giving it a try. I don't know the first thing about making a show horse, but I guess I could learn."

"In nothing flat," said Lisa firmly. "There's really nothing to it if you're a horse person—and if you aren't, nobody is. Once you have the essentials worked out on the flat so that your mount performs with some sort of manners and continuity, than all you have to do is broaden your horizons to take in jumping. Have you done much work over fences, Julie? That can be the only sticky part with a green horse."

"I did do some jumping last summer and fall, after Bonnie's accident, but it was always on somebody else's made horse. I guess it *would* be different with a greenie, but I had a pretty good feeling about it. Enough to think, now, that I'd like to spend some time at it."

"If you decide to give it a try and want some help, just yell. Making hunters is something I do know about." She giggled. "Of course I was sure I knew something about breaking yearlings, too, until I ran into Lights Out. She gave me more trouble than all the other horses I ever broke put together. That's why I sent her to Fieldstone. I knew she had me beat."

Julie nodded, finishing her soda. "She was tough. It was more that nonsense about the bridle than anything else. Once we straightened that out—I mean, Leon did—it was home and dry for her. That reminds me, do you have any wintergreen Life Savers with you?"

Lisa blinked. "No. I like butterscotch myself, if I had any at all. Why?"

"Wait here a minute." Julie went to the counter and came back with a green roll in her hand. "Here, they're for Lights Out."

"What? You're out of your whiffletree."

"I will bet you another soda," said Julie, who was still hungry, "that she'll eat them." Then, thinking of Bonnie and the lime gumdrop, "Even if they *are* green!"

She won.

The rest of that day she spent watching class after class and deluging Lisa with a steady stream of questions about show horses, horse shows, and the general schooling of hunters. Poor Lisa became rather hoarse after a while, but gamely kept explaining. Occasionally they would cross paths with Leon, who was having a grand time renewing old acquaintances. He and Julie agreed to meet by the car at five and head for home. At last that time came, and Julie said goodbye to Lisa and hurried off, while her friend walked off to her trailer to give Lights Out another Life Saver.

As they skirted Meriden, Julie thought suddenly of the Croydon place, but remembering Leon's strong aversion to the subject, she said nothing. An interest in a ghostly-looking old house was all right, if a little childish; but a morbid fascination with the site of two awful murders was inexcusable. She put it out of her mind.

The next couple of weeks passed in a blur, for Julie was deep as ever in her job and, when not actually breaking two-year-olds, spent more time than ever playing with Bonnie, grooming her, feeding her, or simply talking to her quietly. And if she was not by the mare's pasture or in her stall, she would be visiting with Pop and Tweedy—the great Scotch Tweed—in the stallion quarters, or down with Stash and his special protégés, the yearlings. There were twenty-eight of the little demons and Julie had a pet name for each.

Stash was always delighted to have her spend time with the "babies." He would tell her, "Most horse folks don't spend enough time with the young ones, so when it comes up time to break them, they wonder why the critters are wilder than March winds in Ohio. The more they're han-dled, easier it is in the long run for them and us both." Naturally Julie needed no prompting, and thereafter tried to spend part of every afternoon with the colts and fillies. Touching, leading, brushing them; picking up their feet, petting their ears; letting them become familiar with her presence as Stash did.

On the morning when Julie's calendar showed but twelve more days till Bonnie was due to foal, everyone had gathered in the lunchroom. The usual horsemen's conversation that preceded, accompanied, and followed every meal was in full roar. Anecdotes and tales of great horses, all-but-great horses, unlucky horses, dogs of horses, huge bets won and titanic bets lost, detailed accounts of triumphs and tragedies of the horse world, all crossing and mingling and growing somehow more astonishing with each repetition . . .

Julie walked in, and the quick and awkward hush was too obvious not to notice. She looked at Leon, who had just flicked his eyes down at a newspaper. "Is Bonnie all right? Nothing's happened, has it?"

"Everything fine in my quarter," said Leon. "Why you ask, Julie?"

"Don't tell me everything got so quiet because my hem's crooked," said Julie, who was dressed in the inevitable jeans. "I thought it might be Bonnie. You would tell me, wouldn't you, Leon?"

"You think I'd try to keep something about that mare from you?"

"No. I know." Julie blinked. "Sorry, I know better."

"But after you've finished visitin' her this afternoon," said Leon, "instead of coming straight down to the yearling barn, why don't you plan to slip up to the stallion barn and see Pop and Tweedy? And on your way, you might stop by the receiving barn and see—"

"Did the two mares who're booked to Tweedy come in?"

"Yep, they're in. As lovely a pair of mares, barrin' Bonnie, as I ever met. Should come up with something nice from each of them. There's also, ah, a surprise up there for you, Julie."

"A surprise for me!" exclaimed ten-year-old Julie. "What is it, Leon? What is it, Stash? Nat? Ben? Somebody tell me!"

"Nobody knows anything," said Ben, blue eyes wide and innocent.

"Bunch of clams," said Julie hotly. "Pack of ornery sheepherders." She whirled and was gone, to see for herself, not thinking till she was halfway to the car that a surprise told is no surprise.

Stash waited till he heard her car start, then reached for the phone. He dialed three numbers, waited, and one of the lights on the base of the phone flashed on and off, indicating a ringing extension. When the flashing stopped, he said, "On her way. Give her five minutes and we're comin' too." He set down the phone and looked at the grins all around him. "Count down five, then everybody into the pickup. This should be pretty fine!"

Julie reached the receiving barn in three minutes, and that was faster driving than ordinary. She was always careful on the farm, driving very slowly in case of a loose horse or a darting hound. But all horses were either paddocked or stabled at this hour, and the dogs would be napping after lunch, so she felt safe in hustling a little. Thoughts flickered through her mind, but she really couldn't imagine what she'd find in the receiving barn.

As she opened the door, she was confronted with the horse. It was actually Monty Everett and the horse, but since she was hardly expecting to find her old friend there, she literally did not see him at first—only the horse. Then the tall smiling presence registered and she stood glaring at him.

"Don't tell me that Julie Jefferson is at a loss for words," said Monty.

"Montgomery Everett! What are you doing home? You're supposed to be at Kandahar for another week and then ship to Wilshire for the opening day of that meet! Did you get fired?"

"I thought the trainer comes and goes unannounced if he wants to, but if you'd rather, I'll take my friend here and—"

"Oh no!" She took the lead shank from his hand as though he truly might leave with the horse. "Neither of you goes anywhere till I find out who he is, where he came from, what he's doing at Fieldstone—"

"What he had for breakfast—" nodded Monty.

"What you're doing home, and how come everybody on the farm knows something I don't. So you're on, Everett. Make words!"

"I had this free day, see," said Monty patiently. "I

wanted to take a look at that wonky knee on Shadow Boxing. And so the trip wouldn't be lonesome, I brought a pal home with me." He motioned at the big calm gray.

"Whose is he?" she asked, a little quieter.

"He belongs to Julie Jefferson. If she wants him."

For a long moment she was silent and motionless. Then she dropped the lead shank and stretched out both hands toward the horse. Her eyes shone. "You're saying that he's for *me*?"

He stood just short of 16.2 hands high. His steel-gray coat pulled taut across his frame only accentuated his classic lines. Strong bones, an intelligent head, kind but hungry eyes . . .

"Oh, Monty," she said in a whisper. Then she turned to the young man and threw her arms around him and kissed him heartily. "Oh, Monty, thank you! I love him! He's just gorgeous. Oh, how can I ever say thanks enough?"

"You just did," Monty told her. Then the entire lunchroom crew came pouring in the door, just as she kissed him again. They broke into spontaneous applause.

"Pop, Stash, Leon, everybody! Look what Monty brought! Isn't he fantastic?" Then, still holding Monty in a tight hug, "Where did he come from? Why's he so thin? How'd you get him?"

"In the last three days," said Monty, rather breathless and considerably flushed at all this public emotional display, "I've made four trips to absolutely nowhere to acquire a horse we don't really need. A typical Julie Jefferson move if I ever heard of one. Blame it on your influence. Temporary insanity."

"Give me a serious answer, will you?"

"Tell her," said Leon. "No reason to be ashamed of being a decent sort of guy, you know."

"He was on a farm adjacent to the grounds at Kandahar. The man who owned him didn't have much money, and the horse can't run fast enough to pay his own way. So the owner just dumped him at the farm and dropped out of sight. And the manager there wasn't about to give him very much of anything. Afraid of getting stuck for the board bill. That kind of thing gets me where it hurts. If he wasn't going to care for him, why take him at all? Not the horse's fault."

Monty patted the tall gray shoulder. "I kept seeing him on my way to the track in the mornings. Rain or shine, there he was, getting thinner by the minute. Finally I couldn't take it, so I stopped to ask about him. It took me a while to locate the owner and get him bought, but I did, and here he is. Starved, no runner to speak of, but a sweet-tempered and gentle soul. I knew you had to have him. He isn't another Sunbonnet, but . . ."

She had stopped listening to him. Running her hands carefully over the horse, up and down his legs, over his back and quarters, checking for cuts or bruises that might need immediate attention, she was oblivious to everything but the horse.

"His name's Cache," said Monty. "With a *ch*, not an *sh*."

"Uh huh," said Julie, but she never looked up.

Chapter 3

In two days Bonnie was going to foal, according to Julie's meticulous calendar. She was growing more tense by the hour—the girl, not the horse, naturally—and Leon stated firmly that if it hadn't been for Cache and *his* problems, which did occupy a fair amount of Julie's time, she would undoubtedly have driven the whole farm mad. As it was, she was in and out of the mare barn forty times a day, standing at Bonnie's stall door, patting her reassuringly, questioning her with "Bonnie, how do you feel?" and "Are you all right, Bonnie?" and "Bonnie, Bonnie, Bonnie!" until even the great bay mare began to look at her oddly.

Leon was tempted several times to say, "Julie, grow up!" But he didn't, for he knew that the excitement and worry were a part of this girl's veneer and would disappear like smoke in the event of a genuine emergency. Julie would stew like a kettle of catfish that had been left on the stove too long, but let a real problem come up, an incipient calamity show itself, and Julie Jefferson would turn tough and practical and competent far beyond her nineteen years.

However, all the little-girl-with-horsie trimmings that she couldn't help exhibiting while she waited for the overwhelming event, well, they just about sent a fellow loco; or, as Pop Larrikin phrased it, she gave you that old snakes-in-the-boots feeling.

In a coincidental, simultaneous effort to divert her attention, most of the men on the farm made it their business to inquire often about Cache. How was he eating, had he picked up any weight, didn't she think he was

28

looking better, had she ridden him that day? The gray responded gallantly to his role of alternate center of interest. Even though he was second in line for her love, he never seemed to notice. Likely no one had ever showered so much affection on him in all his life before. His personality had been blossoming for ten days now in direct proportion to the amount and quality of feed he consumed. The more he ate, the less he worried about when he might eat again, and at last stopped inhaling every morsel before him as though it might be his last for the month. Then the jokes about his various hollow legs and his pelican-bill stomach died down.

Cache was essentially an extrovert, intrigued by anything around him, inquisitive enough to thrust his nose into places better left alone. So the stable cat left her mark in three sharp lines across his delicate muzzle, while Ben's pet goat butted him soundly on the barrel when he persisted in nibbling her ears. But these small setbacks left him undeterred. He made friends with several of the dogs, including Pushy; but Nana made it plain that she would be superficially courteous and nothing more.

"You don't pick Nana for a pal," Julie told him, "she picks you."

Monty returned that day, hoping to assist in Bonnie's weekend delivery. He spent the better part of the lunch hour catching up on Fieldstone news, and then someone mentioned that the old Croydon place had been sold. This led to a rehashing of the murder story, which was unknown to Monty, and though Leon glared, several of the men took turns describing the old horrors.

"Heard the folks moved in already, too," said Stash. "Pair of 'em, young couple. Heard they have some horses."

"That's nice," said Julie, looking about half there and half in the mare barn. "Do you think Bonnie might want a—"

"Julie," said Leon quickly, "it'd be neighborly to go visit those young people with a sort of welcome basket, wouldn't it?" When the words were out there was no calling them back, and he wondered why he'd said them, feeling as strongly as he did about that old farm. Well, anything to get Julie to leave Bonnie and Fieldstone in peace for an hour or two!

"But Bonnie—"

"Bonniebonniebonnie, you've been grumbling about her for eleven months," said Monty sharply. "The healthiest mare in the whole state. Do you good to get a few miles away from her. Do her good too, from what I hear. Go ask cook to make up a basket. We'll go over to the Croydon spread and help exorcise the ghosts for the new tenants."

"Okay," said Julie meekly, and did so. Shortly the two of them were in the car and on their way. After a mile she said hesitantly, "Have I really been such a pain about Bonnie?"

"I was under-exaggerating," said Monty. "You have the place so jumpy they've started seeing imaginary ailments in that mare where there aren't any. Even Leon's twitchy when you mention her, as you do six times to the minute. I think Stash himself is ready to give you a strong lecture, and if Mr. T heard about it he'd chew your ear. Gently, but chew it. What's wrong with you?"

"I don't know. Ever since she was kidnapped . . ."

"You've treated her as though she were in danger from everything, from viruses and earthquakes and the F.B.I. and I don't know what! That's no way to act, and you know it." He squared his shoulders and clenched the wheel hard. "You listen to what I have to say, Miss Jefferson," he went on, and laid it on her hard. She shrank into the depths of her seat and listened without interruption for a change. When he seemed to be through, she cleared her throat.

"Been that bad, hmm?"

"Yes."

"Pain in the ear."

"In everybody's ear."

"People don't understand how I feel about her."

"That's guff. You understand how I feel about you, but I don't tell you ninety times an hour."

"You don't tell me at all."

"Don't have to, do I?"

She thought. "No."

"Well, then?"

"Oh. Monty," she said in a burst, "I don't even know why you like me. I must be a mess to live with."

"Only when you're agitated about your horse. *Then* you're impossible."

"I'll try to be possible."

"It's against your nature, but try." Unknowingly, he said what Leon had been wanting to tell her. "Grow up some, Julie. You're a big girl now, you know. Bonnie isn't your rag doll, or even old Burglar the raccoon. She's a powerful, tough, healthy horse."

"But fragile," said Julie in a whisper.

"All life is fragile. That doesn't mean we have to worry about everything and everyone we love. Particularly at the tops of our voices."

"You've made your point, boss."

"All right. Onward. Where is this farm?"

"Not far now. You can see the buildings from the road, with a semicircular drive. They look spooky—with good reason."

"Yes, I heard. It's a terrible story. I wonder that someone would buy such a place."

"You don't believe in ghosts?"

"No, but there's bound to be a sadness to the house, to the very grounds. Maybe that's eerie, but since the story's so widely known, well, I don't see how the new owners could escape a chilly feeling."

"That's what I think," said Julie, "and Leon too. We're coming to it now. Turn just after that big sycamore."

The house had been splendid, not ostentatious but sturdy and solid-looking. Its white paint was all but gone, only slivers remaining here and there like pale veins on a dark ground. At first this made it seem totally rundown; yet a second look showed door and windows firmly in place, save for only one broken pane, and a kind of secure appearance. There had been no vandalism here; it was a decent valley, and mischievous children must have been thoroughly warned off this property in the decade and more that it had stood empty. The outbuildings, except for the huge barn that matched the house, were more dilapidated, being flimsier.

Why, then, the ominous impression it made, even from the road, even on people who didn't know its history? Julie couldn't guess.

"You knock," she said to Monty as they ascended the steps, avoiding two that sagged warningly. "I'm scared."

"You expect somebody grim and growly?" asked Monty, lifting his hand. An instant later he decided that he would have been really rather pleased to meet someone grim, for the door opened before he could touch it, and a very handsome man looked out and said, "Oh, hello!" right past him at Julie.

"Hi," said Julie brightly. "We're from Fieldstone Farm, and we heard you'd moved in, and we thought you might need a few things to tide you over the first night or so, and, well, here," she finished, holding the basket forth.

Monty reminded himself that the man who was smiling so broadly was half of a couple, and grinned back, shaking hands with the other man heartily. "Monty Everett of Fieldstone," he said.

"That's a fantastic place," said the man, who was thirty-ish, somewhat taller than Monty, blue-eyed and ruddy-skinned. "I envy you, working there. Tolkov's people are famous for living in luxury and working their hands to the bone. I'm Dirk Markham."

What a romantic name, Julie said to herself, with the corner of one eye on Monty, who, she was aware, was jealous of practically everyone she met except Stash and Pop. "I'm Julie Jefferson," she said.

"Come in, both of you, come in. There's no heat, some very crumbly furniture, a bucket of water from a spring that thank the powers is still sweet and plentiful, and Alexis and me. We were going to go into Meriden for supper, and I didn't want to take the time, so your goodies are a godsend. Is that roast turkey I see under that foil wrap? What a beautiful gesture! Lex! Where are you?"

"We hear that you and your wife brought some horses," said Monty.

Dirk blinked. "I don't have a wife, and we have horses but we haven't brought them here yet. Wait till you see the stables, you'll know why."

"You don't have a wife?"

"I have a sister. I suppose someone saw us together and jumped to thinking I was a cradlerobber. Lex!" he shouted, and took Julie's hand to lead her into the nearest room. "Sit on that chair, the sheet on it's clean. Monty—mind if I call you Monty?—you and I had better stand till Lex brings some more sheets."

"A sister," said Monty, pronouncing the word with reluctance.

"Who on earth discovered we own horses?" asked Dirk.

"A man on Fieldstone who knows almost everything before it happens, including who'll win the Derby," said Julie. "But he goofed on the wife bit. How many horses do you have? Are they thoroughbreds? Do you race?"

He laughed. "No, Croydon isn't going to be in competition with Fieldstone and Deepwater. Ours are hunters and jumpers."

"But they're horses, so you're our kind of people," said Julie.

"I knew a very nice man once who'd never even seen a horse in person," muttered Monty, "and yet he was as real as you could ask for." He winked at Dirk Markham. "Our girl Julie likes horses, you gather. She's the owner of Sunbonnet."

"I've heard the name, but can't place it."

"Sunbonnet, the Bold Ruler filly who won—"

"Julie," said Monty, "there are horse-show people and racing people, and the two worlds don't always overlap. There are *dozens* of people in the world who've never heard of Bonnie."

"I find that hard to believe," said Julie with fervent sincerity.

Dirk clapped his hands with delight. "An enthusiast! That's marvelous."

"Anyway, you're horsey," said Julie, "and I'm pleased, since we'll be so close now. Oh, here's your sister!"

A girl came into the old musty room, a girl as lovely in her slight, dark fashion as Dirk was handsome. Her eyes were enormous and green, and her face, though narrow, was magnificently boned. She looked at them and nodded uncertainly.

"Lex, this is Julie Jefferson and Monty Everett of Fieldstone. My sister Alexis. They brought us all sorts of life-saving edibles."

"That was very good of you," said the girl; her voice was low and level. "I've eaten in one too many restaurants to be thrilled by dining out any longer."

"Roast turkey's in this basket," said Dirk.

"Thank you!" said Alexis with a flash of a smile at Monty. "That makes the day."

"How many horses do you have?" asked Julie, and the other girl started, as strangers were apt to do until they became accustomed to her major preoccupation.

"Lex has six and I have five," said Dirk.

"Great! When are you bringing them?"

"When I have the stable ready. It's a wreck, the only absolute wreck on the place. The roof fell in about 1965, I think. I may have to rebuild entirely. But the kennels are in good shape."

"Oh, dogs too?"

"Only ten couple of hounds at the moment, but I want more."

Julie gave an exclamation of delight. "I must bring Nana to meet them!"

"You must not," said Monty. "Blasted beagle," he explained to the Markhams, "eats nothing but Persian leather, Oriental carpets, and Ming vases."

"My kind of beast," said Dirk to Julie. "Bring her by all means. Have you any show horses at Fieldstone?"

"Not yet," said Julie, as Monty gave her a startled stare. "When you said your hunters and jumpers weren't racers, you didn't mean they weren't thoroughbreds?"

"Oh, no, of course they are. I'm afraid we aren't very well informed about racehorses and the kind of breeding that you two see every day. By and large, our horses are those that have failed at the track, for if they *could* run, their value'd lie in racing, not showing. Our greatest pleasure comes from schooling them to jump, and showing's simply a measure of our progress."

"Showing is just as important as racing," said Alexis quietly. "And maybe neither one is very important in the scheme of things, but I wouldn't trade with anyone, even the owner of Sunbonnet."

"You know about Julie's horse?" asked Dirk, looking surprised.

"I heard you speak of her. I recognized the name. I remember when she was hurt. Tough luck."

"She's mended well, and she's almost ready to foal for the first time," Monty said.

"You must be on pins and needles," said Dirk to Julie sympathetically.

"Razor blades and daggers," grunted Monty. He was torn between a feeling of liking for this man and a distinct impression that he was too good-looking and hearty and horsey to trust around Julie.

That young lady, fresh from her long day with Lisa Marsden and therefore superficially knowledgeable on the subject, continued to question Dirk (*why not Alexis?* thought Monty with unusual venom) on show horses, and Dirk responded to her interest with increasing ease and volubility; in fact, he talked almost as fluently and briskly as Julie herself. Monty fidgeted. Alexis stood silently, watching her brother.

"No," Dirk said in answer to a query, "it's not uncommon for two or three of our protégés to be among the high-score champions of their respective divisions each year, if I can brag among friends."

"Then how many horses are you showing now?"

"Only six. Lex has four and I have two. My strip colt— conformation colt, you know—popped a splint about a month ago, and I've laid him up for the rest of the year. Hated to do it, but if I can get it off him without firing or making too much of a mess, he can stay in the division. Otherwise we'll have to go working with him next year, where 'beauty' isn't counted in your score."

"And how often do you show your horses, and where do you go with them?"

"Just about every weekend, though we don't take all the horses every time. We stagger them, so they don't get sour. Where? Any place on the east coast. Last month, for instance, we were in Florida for the Sunshine Circuit and spent a week apiece in Ocala, South Miami, and Delray Beach. There's a break of two weeks now before we go again, and then it'll be Middleburg, Warrenton, and on to Pennsylvania for two."

"Oh, wow!" said Julie. "You just rattled off every major horse show in the "A" circuit as if it was a backyard gymkhana. Do your horses win enough in that company to make all that travel worth your while?"

She had not meant to be insulting, or to pry. She was simply amazed to hear him talk so casually about the biggest, most competitive shows in the country. She would have spoken the same way a year ago about Bonnie, but then Bonnie had been one of the most marvelous money-makers of that time.

"We've been lucky," said Dirk easily. "Our horses are pretty consistent. And Lex," he added, giving his sister a warm smile and letting a tone of frank admiration come into his voice, "she's very talented in schooling over fences; hunters or jumpers, it doesn't matter, they're all the same to her. She's terrific."

"Not all that great," said Alexis, her thin face flushing with pleasure—or embarrassment.

"Fact. Her brown mare, November Witch, was green-hunter high-score champion last year, and is leading the open and amateur/owner divisions this year. She'll be happy to show her to you as soon as the work on the barn is finished and we bring the horses here."

"How long will that be?" asked Monty.

"As fast as I can get the barn-repair crew to work. Lord knows. But I want Croydon to be perfect as quickly as possible."

"You'll call it Croydon, then."

Dirk nodded slowly. "Out of respect for the original family, I believe that's only right. Are you thinking of the taint of old horror, or the ghosts, or the scandal?"

"No," said Monty in some confusion. "I think you're being very decent to keep the old name."

"I couldn't do less."

"What about *your* horses?" Julie asked him, drawing the conversation back to essentials. "Are they on a par with November Witch?"

Dirk chuckled. Alexis said, "Dirk's too modest, so he brags about me. He's been champion at four out of five shows with his preliminary jumper, and he's won two grand prix jumping classes with his open horse."

Julie made a mental note to check some horse publications, for she began to realize that the Markhams were "somebody" in their world. Perhaps she'd ask Lisa about them. Monty, strictly a racehorse man, tapped his foot nervously.

"Tell me about Croydon," he said at random. "What will you do with it? Farm generally, or make it strictly equine-supporting?"

"The latter," said Dirk. "We'll have the barns and kennels readied first, naturally, then the fence lines; finally the house and the outbuildings. Next time you come I hope we can all four sit down!"

"I apologize, I should have found some more sheets," said Alexis.

"Trainers are used to standing," said Monty. He glanced around him, almost said that it was a shadowy, spectral old place, and swallowed the words with an audible gulp.

Dirk, who always appeared to be addressing both of them but looked mainly at Julie, said, "You mentioned not having any show horses at Fieldstone yet. Does that mean you're thinking of making some?"

"No indeed," said Monty.

"Yes," said Julie eagerly at the same time. "I have a new horse, a wonderful horse but not fast enough for the track, and I've been thinking I'd like to school him"—blithely ignoring Monty's popped eyes—"but I can't do

it alone, for I wouldn't really be sure what I was doing.
I have a fair idea of what they *should* go like, but how you
go about getting them there is brand-new and a mystery
to me. This horse, he's a gray, is one of the most athletic
animals I've ever ridden, and a super mover. I think he
could jump the moon if he wanted to, but I'll settle for
three-foot-six till I know what we're both doing."

"Cache a show horse?" said Monty.

"Well, he failed racing, but he's strong and willing and
I know he can do it!"

"I'll help you," said Dirk. "So will Lex, won't you,
dear?"

The dark and green-eyed girl nodded slowly, moving a
step or two closer to her brother, but watching Julie.

"Listen, we've stayed longer than we meant," Monty
said a shade too loudly. "You have work to do and we're
holding it up."

"Not at all," said Dirk.

"Promise you'll come to Fieldstone soon and meet
Bonnie and her foal and look at Cache?"

"Julie, we'll be there before the foal's dry," said Dirk.

They all moved out to the door in a flurry of goodbyes,
and the Fieldstone couple felt the crisp cool air like a
welcome to the world after the closeness of the house.
When they had driven onto the main road again, Monty
said quietly, "You might have told me your plans for
Cache first, you know, instead of blurting them out to the
first handsome stranger you ran into."

"Oh, I'm sorry, Monty," she said, contrite. "They never
jelled till now. Besides, he's not a stranger, he's a neighbor
and a friend."

"His sister's a funny sort, isn't she? Did you catch
something slightly, well, hostile in her manner?"

"You imagine things," said Julie. "After all, she's very
young, and probably shy with new people."

"Must be nearly a year younger than you are," said
Monty.

"She's very pretty, isn't she?"

Monty shrugged. "Not much prettier than a movie

actress." With that one, he began to whistle a tuneless tune, while Julie regarded him with one raised eyebrow. But he didn't refer to the girl Alexis again, and Julie wouldn't.

Chapter 4

When the big bay showed no sign of foaling by Sunday night, Monty returned to the track, leaving the entire farm in a state of watchful expectancy. No one but he knew why Julie herself was so much less vocal and jumpy about it, and Monty was not quite sure whether it was his lecture or dreams of Dirk that kept the blond girl calmer than usual. He could only hope, he thought ruefully as he drove away, that the stern words had taken root.

"After all," Julie was then explaining patiently to Leon, "a mare doesn't have to be on schedule, eleven months to the day, now does she? That would be unnatural!"

"Right," said Leon, polishing his glasses and gazing at her with wonder. "I'm glad you told me. I might have taken alarm."

"Happy to tranquilize your fears," said Julie, going off to bite her knuckles in privacy.

On Tuesday the Markhams came over to visit in mid-afternoon. They toured Fieldstone thoroughly, Julie acting as guide. When they were back to where they'd started, having met every horse and man on the place, Dirk said warmly, "I feel as familiar with your place now as I do with Croydon. Could draw the layout in my sleep. Fascinating! I've never seen such a magnificent spread of land. I'm glad we're so near, aren't you, Lex?"

"Of course we're away a great deal of the time," said his sister, who seemed to have been impressed only twice, once by Bonnie and once by Cache, thus endearing herself to Julie.

"As to Cache," went on the young man, "I'd say he's a fine prospect for what you have in mind, Julie. I'll be glad to help with his schooling, won't you, Lex?"

"I'll do what I can," said Alexis. "I don't want to intrude."

"Intrude!" Julie was vehement. "You come and go as you like. You're family now!"

Dirk laughed. "Julie, you're marvelous at making people feel at home. We'll *do* that." He furrowed his brows thoughtfully. "I've meant to ask before, would you be interested in fox hunting?"

"Fox hunting?" repeated Julie in a crescendo. "Chase a poor defenseless innocent beautiful fox with a pack of big dogs? Me?"

"'The unspeakable in pursuit of the inedible' is how the quotation goes. I don't mean with a real fox; you needn't hunt them at all, you know, and actually I like to watch the hounds work and feel the horse go, that's the sport of it. I'd like to start a drag hunt in the area if I can drum up enough interest. I thought you might be willing to introduce me to some of the farm owners so that I can get their reactions to the notion. And I hoped you might want to ride with us."

"A drag hunt," said Alexis scornfully. "Almost as exciting as chasing a boy on a bicycle."

"Better than no hunt at all, and less blood and death in the world," said Dirk equably.

Julie knew that in a drag hunt, a rider is sent out a few hours ahead of the pack, towing a heavily scented, inanimate sack which lays a trail for the hounds to follow. That made everything all right. "I'd adore it," she said. "When your hounds are here and you're ready, we'll go visiting, I promise."

"Good! Come over to Croydon when you have the chance, and let us know when Bonnie's foaled."

That, it seemed, would not be soon. Day after day, night after night, then a second *week,* and she still showed no sign of desiring to present the universe with an exquisite, shaky little replica of herself.

"She gets bigger and bigger," said Julie plaintively to Stash, "but nothing happens!"

"Why should a baby horse leave the protection of his mama and face this complexified business of livin' any sooner's absolutely necessary? You know they're unpredictable. Just leave it to Bonnie."

"I am, Stash, I am. Haven't I been good about it?"

"Yes you have, and your daddy'd be proud of you. Mature," said Stash gravely, "that's the word I want for you. Mature. Good word. Good state, long as you don't take it too serious."

"I feel anything but," said Julie. "I feel about two feet high and helpless as a turtle on its back."

"She'll be endin' the suspense as soon as she's prepared for it," he said comfortingly.

It had been ten days or more since she'd visited Pop and Tweedy at the stallion barn, and her daily trips to play with the yearlings had also ceased. Her work itself did not suffer; Julie would have had to be confined to bed before she'd have neglected that. But all the other hours when she was not sleeping like the dead she was keeping vigil outside Bonnie's stall. Though Leon made it his custom to pass through the barn every hour, she had twice roused him from his cot to be sure some symptom was not a sign of approaching motherhood. She had never actually witnessed the birth of a foal, and was not fully familiar with the various behavior patterns of brood mares come to their time. Stash, Leon, even the vet Dr. Haffner, had drilled into her (now that she would sit still and listen) all that they could call to mind of the subject; but there are so many variations, such multitudes of differences among mares, that she could never be sure whether a quirky little trick was a genuine symptom or a nothing-whatever.

And when Haffner told her a mare might conceivably carry a foal anywhere from two to four weeks beyond the calculated date, she really doubted that her nervous system would survive.

Bandicoot and Petal had foaled earlier in the month, but in the late morning while Julie was still working, so she had missed the spectacle of birth and had to content herself with the miracle of a wobbly-legged baby, less than half an hour old, trying desperately to stand on his feet . . . and making it.

Time loitered on, and it was within forty-eight hours of being a twelve-month foal. Julie had arrived at the brood-mare barn. Leon, long since abandoning his diversionary tactics of useless chores and extra busywork to fill the empty spaces of life, had produced a checkerboard and three decks of cards instead. Bales of straw served for chairs and tables, and nearly everyone on the farm stopped by at one time or another for a quick hand or two or a chance at the checkers. Young Tim McChrystal, who spent his mornings schooling two-year-olds with Julie and his afternoons attending art classes, had made a big sign announcing that this was LEON'S ESTABLISHMENT—Casino Très Extraordinaire! Stash contributed a green-visored dealer's cap, one pinochle deck, and a stack of hand-drawn score cards.

"Hi, Julie," Leon greeted her cheerfully that afternoon. "How's it going?"

"Pretty good. Even the flop-eared chestnut's acting as if he had some sense. Anything I can do?"

"Nothin' in the line of work. I have to fix this hay rack in Mimi's stall, got her almost done, then how about we pick up that gin rummy game we left the other day? If you haven't shredded up the score card by now?"

"I was losing badly, but I'll do better today. Couldn't do worse if I—Leon!" She had slid open the door to Bonnie's stall and found it empty. She looked around in disbelief, as though she could have missed seeing a pregnant horse. "Where is she? She's gone! She's not out with the other mares, because I came up through that field. Do you suppose something's—"

"Don't say it!"

"—happened to her?"

"Whoa up, hold it right there! She's in the sun paddock today so I can keep an eye on her. You had to walk right past her when you came in from that end of the barn."

"Never looked there. You think she'll foal today, then."

"Sometime within the next twenty-four, don't know exactly when."

"Why? She's been bagged up for simply weeks, and still no baby!"

Leon laughed. "Well, honey, getting the milk bar filled and ready for business is one of nature's ways of letting us know that something's momentarily gonna happen. When you look at her today you'll see little waxy beads have formed on the ends of her teats, and the muscles between the point of her croup and her hip have conspicuously relaxed so there's a definite hollow where there wasn't one before. Nature's telling us that the time's at hand."

Finished with the hay rack, he came to her side. "The muscles relax to allow an easier passage for the foal. The little drops of beads are colostrum, that'll be the baby's first milk. It's important that a foal gets it pretty quick after it's born; it has all the what-d'you-call-'ems, the immunizations it needs for its first days of life."

"What do we do if the foal can't or doesn't get the colostrum?" asked the girl, distressed by a mental image of a newborn foal unable to nurse.

"If the mare's kind and she'll let down her milk, then we milk her into a baby bottle and feed the foal that way. But if the mare says no—and some of the best of 'em do— then you have to go to formulas and feeding schedules and hope that the foal will take a man-made substitute. *And* will drink from a bottle."

"Oh wow, I never even thought about that kind of problem. I was too worried about her having the baby. I knew that anything but the two normal foaling presentations meant big trouble, that you could lose the mare or the foal or both . . . but I don't like to think about terrible things like that, and I guess I believed that once it was safely born, the problems were over."

Leon nodded, watching the frown of concentration. He knew that she was reviewing everything she'd just learned and filing it carefully under "Foals" for future reference. She turned and walked down the aisle, deep in thought, stopped at the door, and turned back. "Hey, Leon," she said, "I sure am glad that you're here to take care of Bonnie." The door closed quietly behind her.

Julie spent the best part of an hour with her mare in the sun paddock. For the first time since she had been

rescued, a taut bag of bones, from the river in Spire's
Yard, Bonnie responded with less than total attention.
She was restless, quiet, restless again, walking the fence
line, stopping in a far corner to stare motionless into
space. She was not intrigued with grazing, nor would she
pick at the pile of fresh-cut clover that Leon had put there
for her. This was all so uncharacteristic of the mare that
Julie finally decided she'd prefer to be left alone, and
unwillingly trailed off once more.

In the barn she reported to Leon, and pulling out the
straw bales, cards, and score pad, declared that the casino
was open.

She ordinarily played an excellent game of cards, bold
and speedy, but the game that had started so badly was
slated to end the same way. Her mounting anticipation and
apprehension prevented concentration on the cards. She
lost seven straight hands and twice discarded her own gin
card, before deciding that the game was hopeless.

"Just one more hand," said Leon, "then it's time for
afternoon chores anyhow." He shuffled. "We'll do up the
barn for the evening after you win this'n."

She was sorting her hand when Pushy wandered in and
eased alongside her. Absently she patted his great head,
asked where he'd been, and began to play. The gentle
saint waited quietly beside her for several minutes, then
with a blubbery sigh and a glance of mournful apology
for the interruption, gravely placed one cut and bloodied
forepaw on her knee.

"Pushy! What ever happened? Your poor paw!" Gently
she lifted the bleeding leg and inspected it from elbow to
toes. "Oh, you've just missed the tendon! This needs
sutures as soon as possible, Leon. I don't think Haffner
would touch it, I'm taking Push to town. Will you call Doc
Sims and say I'm coming?"

"Sure thing, but first let me stop some of the bleedin'
with a pressure bandage. Whatever did it, it missed the
artery, but sure made a mess." He had reached in the wall
box as he spoke and produced gauze, cotton for padding,
and an elastic bandage. Deftly he arranged the cotton
and gauze, bound them on. "That'll hold till you get to

Sims. Be brave, my man," he said formally to Pushy, who hobbled awkwardly behind Julie with his throbbing paw held aloft in the casing.

Leon was somewhat late with his afternoon chores, but not being a clockwatcher, was surprised to see Stash Watkins come through the door while he was still mixing the grain. They exchanged greetings as Stash ambled over to have a look at Bonnie. He agreed that she'd foal soon, and then realized that Julie wasn't in the barn. Leon told him about Pushy's accident.

"That's kind of outlandish, Leon. That old pup is the carefullest critter on this farm. How'd he go to get sliced up? That does make me wonder."

"Me too. Finish feedin', I'm taking a run to Julie's cottage. I didn't mention it to her, and she's all distracted, but I'd lay eight to five she left both her dogs inside today."

"Why you so positive?"

"The rat poison that's down where they're remodeling the feed-storage building. Julie keeps the dogs with her when they're out, till that construction's finished she'll do that, and the poison's covered all safe again. Today wouldn't be any exception, no matter how much her mind's on Bonnie there."

"Lemme help you with that feedin'," said Stash. "Yeah. Go ahead with what you were mountin' up to, Leon."

"How did Pushy get down here, and better yet, what was in that house to hack him up so fierce? Where's that scatterbrained beagle, who's out if Push is? Makes no sense. Nobody opens the door of that house when Julie's not there, you know that."

"Let's get these brood mares supplied," said Stash. "I'm with you."

They fed the thirty-odd mares in record time. When they stepped out of the old truck at Julie's cottage, the kitchen door stood wide and jagged pieces of glass were strewn across the floor, some with red smears on them. "Not hard to deduce what cut him. Wonder what it was, and how it got busted?"

"Where's the rattleheaded beagle? Let's get this mess tidied," said Leon.

"Put all the pieces in a paper sack," said Stash, scratching his jaw in deep thought. Don't miss none with red on 'em."

"Sweep it into the garbage, man!"

"Nope. Save it. I got my reasons."

"As you say, old man," sighed Leon, reaching down a thick grocery bag. "What's in your mind?"

"Tell you, ancient one. Just you touch that big curved chunk there, touch the blood on it."

Leon did so. "Dry already. That's funny, oldtimer."

"That's more'n funny, my antique buddy. That's impossible. Dry blood turns brown. That's scarlet. That ain't Pushy's blood, that's paint. And no dog stands around bleedin' all over what's sliced him; he jumps back, leaves no more'n a drop or two. I want to fit these pieces together. Because, you poor old decrepit veteran you, you know well as I that Julie keeps absolutely *nothin'* in this house that could fall and bust and hurt a dog."

Leon whistled soundlessly. "You have got something there, even if you are so aged your brains creak when the wheels go round. And the pups would have been in this kitchen, too, 'cause Nana lost her run-o'-the-house privileges after she ate that quilt. Hold on a second! Pushy would have been in there. Julie said it yesterday; kitchen's too small for Push to sprawl around comfortable-like, so she puts the beagle here and gives Push the rest of the place!"

"Go see is there another door open, while I collect this sharp stuff," said Stash, getting onto his knees with the bag.

Leon went swiftly through the cottage. "Only the kitchen door," he said, returning.

"Doors. One to the outside, one to the dining room. That's funny too, if Nana's supposed to be in a jail cell here by herself."

"Curious!"

"Worse'n that. I don't care for it a smidgin, Leon. Too much mystery for me. I only hope Julie is too converged on Bonnie's condition to think much about how Pushy got cut and out. We have to locate that blame beagle, too, you know."

"A job for the Marines," Leon said sadly. However, before they had swept up the last of the glass shards Nana appeared at the door, dusty and panting and wagging her hindquarters irrepressibly. They snapped a leash on her collar and anchored her to a chair until the floor was safe again; then they renewed a spilt water-bowl and left her the run of the kitchen. She slouched wearily to her pile of blankets and towels and collapsed in a weary heap of dog.

"Where's she been? What was she after?" remarked Leon unhappily. "Wish she could talk."

"She can to some extenuation. That dust came from Ogden's Mill Road." That was the back way into the farm, opposite Route 143. "Tar and cinder dust—road, not field or woods. That means no rabbits for a change."

They stared at each other. "Car?" ventured Leon.

"Sure as little horse pills. A car. And a long way, too. Let's get up to the barn where you can watch Bonnie and Southern Cross."

"And Rushlight. I got my doubts about her."

"And I'll put my nimble fingers to work on reconstructin' this glass hullabaloo. I have a fierce wish to see what in the name of Mr. Holmes it was before it got crunched."

"Mr. Holmes?" said Leon as they closed the door firmly and went to the truck.

"Shylock Holmes, you ignorant old man," said Stash loftily. "The greatest detective of 'em all."

"Oh, him," said Leon.

Stash got some high-strength clear cement and a good spot under a light, and carefully dumped all the glass onto a piece of board across a straw bale; then he sat down and began to piece the object together laboriously, while Leon alternately watched him and checked the mares. After a while, he whistled long and pensively.

"What you so tuneful about?" demanded Leon, back from one of his frequent visits.

"You see what this was? Comin' clear now."

"What is?"

"This object de art, which is what they call stuff that sits around waitin' to get broke."

"Well, what was it?"

"Ask me in ten minutes."

"I'll do that." Which, checking his watch, he did.

"A hatchet. A glass hatchet. Like maybe for George Washington Carver's birthday, you know?"

"That was Washington, you noodle, not Carver. What about the red?"

"Paint, smeared on the blade of it. Hatchet was hollow 'n' kinda thin, or it wouldn't have smashed like that."

"I'll be dipped in liniment," said Leon, and abandoned their light banter abruptly. "A bloody axe, Stash. Does that remind you of anything?"

"Nothing much. What should it?"

"Croydon."

"Why?"

"Maybe you haven't heard all the old story. The old couple who were murdered by their son . . ."

"Spit it out, Leon."

"Were killed with something like an axe. Never found, but the coroner said that was the weapon."

They stared at each other in the naked glow of the big light bulb.

"Mystery on mystery."

"Not nice."

"No. Keep it from Julie till we find out what's up."

"Right."

They solemnly shook hands, while the shattered axe with its streaks of red paint gleamed between them.

It was past nine in the evening when Julie came back to the barn. Dr. Sims had used a general anesthetic for the deep sutures and she had waited until Pushy was awake enough to be comforted by her voice and then to drift off into a heavy, relaxed sleep. The vet would keep him at the hospital for a few days, to be sure that he didn't chew the stitches out and that his wound was healing properly. She eased noiselessly into the darkened stable, her sneakered feet making no sound on the slip-proof asphalt, and peered into her bay's stall through the small viewing square set into the side. In the rosy glow of the infrared lights built into the ceiling of every stall, she saw that Bonnie looked perfectly normal. A quick glance at her luminous watch dial told her that Leon would be here on his hourly round almost at once, so she waited, watching Bonnie. She was more than a little astonished when twenty minutes had fled before he appeared. He moved quickly from stall to stall, as silent as Julie had been, making sure all was in order. He waved a silent hello to the girl, put his finger to his lips, and beckoned.

As they stepped out into the archway that connected the two halves of the brood-mare barn, he spoke with resignation. "Never rains but we have a flood, honey. Tonight's fixed to be a humdinger! How's old Pushy?"

"Fine. What's happening?"

"Nothing exactly bad, at least not yet, more like inconvenient. Three mares are foaling tonight."

"Ouch!"

"Yes, all in various stages, at opposite ends of the barn, and it looks like that brown mare, Rushlight, is about three weeks early and may be in for a hard time. Doc's just gone out for a quick sandwich, he'll be right back."

Her pulse accelerated. "Who are the other two? Is Bonnie one?"

"She is." Leon gave her a wry smile. "I was almost positive of that this afternoon. Then Rushlight started showing signs of early labor a while back, after ignorin' her supper. But the real shocker was making the eight o'clock to find Southern Cross running milk. She'd already been down a couple of times by the look of her stall. Older mares can fool you. One minute nothing, next minute bagged up, muscles slacked, foal all but on the ground! I've seen it so many times you'd think I'd be used to it, predict it. But she caught me napping." He took her arm. "Bonnie's not ready, so you come over and see what's happening."

Reluctantly but curiously, she followed him into the other half of the barn.

As the night wore on, every time Julie began to relax something happened. With Bonnie, though, all remained peaceful. She began to wonder whether Leon might be mistaken about her mare. Maybe tomorrow, she thought; that would make it easier for the vet and Leon and Julie herself.

Rushlight, as the foreman had feared, had a difficult time. Julie was impressed afresh by the skill and wisdom evidenced by Leon and Dr. Haffner, who spent a harrowing twenty minutes together delivering the foal.

Since Caesarian section is rarely performed on horses, in order for a foal to be born without complications it must start down the birth canal in one of two "normal" positions. In the more common of these, the foal somewhat resembles a diver with its forelegs extended in front of its body, its nose resting atop the forelegs, and the hindquarters extended behind it. This is nature's way of ensuring that the foal will pass through the canal as easily as possible. The other normal position is the direct reverse of this one.

However, time becomes the deciding factor. After the foal enters the birth canal, the pressure of the mare's contractions is so great as to cut off the circulation through the umbilical cord, which means that the foal must soon begin breathing on its own. So only fifteen or twenty minutes are available in which to produce a live foal, once the process has begun; for beyond that time the foal will die of suffocation.

If a foal is so jammed up inside the mare that it cannot be righted quickly enough to be born alive, then all efforts must go toward saving the mare by getting the foal out. It is possible for a mare to continue in labor for one and a half, even two hours before shock, exhaustion, toxic shock, or other complications will claim her life. So, once it becomes plain that the mare cannot produce a live foal, the general procedure is for the vet to go inside and dissect the foal to remove it.

Suddenly, as she thought of these facts and watched Leon and Doc at work, she realized that without such dedicated people, foaling would be a dreadfully hazardous matter. How many tragedies must have occurred when most horses ran wild! But with competent attendants and a resident vet, there is almost no reason ever to lose a mare, and the percentage of foals born alive is greatly increased.

The brown mare Rushlight was in trouble almost from the start, when her first contractions produced only one foreleg and a nose. This meant that the other foreleg was either folded back at the knee or lying under the foal's body from the shoulder. The latter proved to be the case, and to straighten this leg the foal had to be pushed back inside the mare and the leg manipulated into position. This was far from easy, for the mare's continuing contractions made it a test of strength as well as skill. Just as Julie was ready to give up hope of seeing a live foal, Doc pulled it from the mare and stepped back to catch his breath. The mare lay, exhausted, on the straw, her coat shining black with sweat, her breath laboring in brief gasps, her eyes closed—but her baby was alive! The foal was a colt, though he more nearly resembled a half-drowned lamb than anything equine, and of course Julie loved him instantly.

During all the excitement that followed the birth, Julie told Leon she could be of some use if she made his rounds instead of standing outside the stall like a gaping schoolgirl, and took off. Southern Cross seemed to have settled a little from her previous up-and-down enterprise, while Bonnie, for the first time since the afternoon in the sun paddock, was growing restless, and had begun systematically to lick the walls of her stall with ferocious dedication. Having just seen an example of the problems that could arise, Julie was overwhelmed by the fear that Bonnie might soon find herself in a plight similar to that of the brown mare.

Back at Rushlight's stall, Leon was briskly rubbing the colt with Turkish towels, and told Julie that the mare was far too tired to dry him properly and that he, Leon, was just helping out till she felt better. Instinct and recuperative powers being what they are, he assured the girl that by the time the little fellow was able to stand on his feet and nurse, the mare would be up too.

Another check disclosed Bonnie alternately walking the

perimeter of the stall and washing the walls. Her nostrils were dilated and her sides had begun to heave ever so slightly. Though Julie did her best to disguise it, her mounting fear for Bonnie was plainly printed across her face when she came back to Leon. He assured her that there was no reason to anticipate any trouble at all; he knew better than to make light of it, for the bond between girl and mare was very special indeed, but he tried to allay her dread with logic, explaining that thoroughbreds have a pretty good batting average and that thousands of foals are born to them every year with no complications whatever.

As they stood now outside Bonnie's stall, Julie watching her big beast in silence, the first rivulets of sweat began to trace down across the glossy coat. Leon prayerfully willed the mare to get on with it, to have a good foal easily, so that the girl could have some peace of mind. They were so intent on their private thoughts that neither of them heard Stash till he stood directly behind them.

"Southern Cross 'll drop her foal any minute now," he whispered.

"Right. Come on, Julie. Bonnie's still okay and you ought to see a real pro at work."

"Who?" She had just seen a real pro, Doc Haffner.

"Southern Cross. Come along."

She was a fragile-looking mare. She had always reminded Julie of a porcelain figurine: perfect in every detail, but utterly breakable. However, Southern Cross was an example of looks being deceiving, for after a brilliant racing career as a top stakes mare, she'd produced five exceptional foals of the highest racing caliber.

Julie hesitated. She didn't really want to leave Bonnie. But Stash and Leon knew best. She followed them once again to the opposite end of the huge barn.

In less than a dozen minutes, the little mare had waited stoically through three powerful contractions, chosen her foaling spot in the straw, and without any ado lay down and produced a colt as easily as a tree produces spring buds. She lay on the straw no longer than it took Julie to

exclaim softly over her feat, then stood and set to work
at the motherly chore of drying her baby.

"Quite a night for colts," Stash said, as Doc Haffner
dabbed iodine on the stump of the umbilical cord. "S'pose
Bonnie's going to give us a boy too."

"This little mare never fails to birth a beauty," said
Leon, watching her with a professional eye to spot the
least sign of anything wrong, as Julie stared as the minutes-
old foal struggled to gain his feet. Then he let out his first
shrill foal-whinny, and Julie laughed aloud with delight.

If only Bonnie would do as well, have as easy a time!

Chapter 5

"Well, everything here is just fine," said Doc. "I'm going back with Rushlight; that baby might need some help getting started. Leon, shout if you need me at your end."

He headed for the brown mare, while Julie and her two old friends returned to Bonnie. They arrived barely in time to catch the great bay lying down and, as Julie watched in awe, there appeared two forefeet, a nose, and then, wonder of wonders, the entire foal!

"Talk about old pros," said Stash, "I'd admire to see an easier birthin' than *that*!"

But when ten minutes had passed and the mare still lay on the straw, her sides heaving as if in continued labor, Leon stepped inside to cauterize the cord and begin drying the infant with a towel. A quick glance from him and a nod sent Stash running for the veterinarian, while Julie's joy at the newborn life crumbled into silent, panicky terror for her mare. What could be wrong? She would have leaped to Bonnie's side, but she was paralyzed.

Doc appeared on the double, sized up things, pulled on his arm-length plastic glove and knelt to reach inside the laboring mare. He probed in silence for a minute, and Julie became aware of the wheezing and gasping of the evidently tormented horse; then he looked around at her with a triumphant grin.

"Julie!" he said.

"What?" numbly.

"It's twins!"

Julie could not speak.

"I'll be blessed," said Doc reverently. "I never suspected. Let's hang tough for a few minutes and see if she can get this one out by herself. If not, I'll bring it."

Gasps and exclamations, then, that nobody heard and nobody knew they were uttering. Leon shook his head in disbelief, continuing his ministrations. Then he said, "This one's a colt, if anyone cares just now."

With the minimum assistance from the vet, Bonnie foaled the second baby, a small and terribly weak-looking filly. The three men exchanged long looks, then all turned to Julie, but no one spoke till the girl demanded, "Why are you all staring at me? Is there something I ought to do, or say? Bonnie's all right *now,* isn't she? Or is it triplets?"

"Over to you, Doc," said Leon.

"Well, ah, Julie, twins—twins very rarely make it in the racing world. You're lucky, because the colt's exceptionally large for a twin, he's about on a par with any other good newborn foal. But the filly . . ."

"Well, she's a little wobbly, and small—"

"Very tiny indeed. Not strong at all, either. She really hasn't got anything going for her, Julie. It would be best if she were destroyed now, instead of bothering her with being raised into a nothing, a weakling, if she'd survive at all."

"Destroy her! Oh no, you can't do that! I'll take care of her myself," said Julie, all but shouting. She ran into the stall and snatching at one of Leon's towels, began drying the little creature as she'd seen him do with the others. "You won't touch a hair of her," she said between her teeth. "No, no, no!"

Bonnie, on her feet now, appeared to sense the girl's sudden desperation, and as though to protect both girl and filly, placed her great body menacingly between them and the three men. And there is nothing more menacing in the world than a large and angry mother. Even Leon stepped back a few paces.

"All right," said the vet, "both of you win. I'll not harm your baby! But let me iodine that cord." He moved toward Julie and the filly, a cotten swab soaked with iodine in his outstretched hand. Savagely Bonnie closed her teeth on his wrist, making him drop the swab and jerk his arm back in pained surprise. "I can take a hint. You'll have to do it, Julie, all of it, beginning with cauterizing that cord."

Julie did as she was told, secretly delighted that Bonnie would allow no one else to touch her tiny filly foal. The colt himself was up within the hour, teetering and tottering on his not-yet-hardened hoofs, stumbling and falling backward and forward, always trying again. Julie touched the fragile filly, wishing fervently that she too would get to her feet. Far within herself, Julie knew that keeping this one alive would be a long shot. But she knew that all her friends would help her as best they could, and hoped that they could do enough. . . .

From that first night on, Bonnie made it evident that only Julie Jefferson would be tolerated near her sickly baby, and although the men were allowed to inspect the colt as they wished, the filly was strictly taboo. In about an hour, Leon produced a baby bottle and told the girl to fill it with the colostrum and to feed the filly her first meal. Bonnie, luckily, cooperated generously, and soon the filly was happily suckling away. The colt behaved much as any other newborn foal, and when his first appetite was satisfied, sank into the fresh straw to sleep off the exhaustion of being born. Julie waited until the filly had taken as much from the bottle as she would and was breathing rhythmically in slumber, then quietly backed away and took her first careful look at the colt.

His coat was almost dry, and stood away from his little body in the typical foal-fuzz way. It was hard to tell just what color he'd eventually be—they wouldn't know for sure until he lost his baby coat—but from his light mane and tail, he seemed to favor his sire and would be a chestnut like Tweedy. A tiny white star was his only evident marking. As he slept dreamlessly there on the straw, Julie knew absolutely that he was destined for greatness. After all, with Sunbonnet and Scotch Tweed for parents, how could he fail? She wished she could be as sure about the filly; but if determination and the will to succeed counted for anything, then the filly would not face life without a hope.

She gave Bonnie a bear hug, complimented the weary mare on her two lovely children, and stepped out of the stall to learn about the care and feeding of her tiny charge.

Doc outlined the feeding schedule for her, which would begin with a bottle every half hour or so. If the filly seemed hungry at shorter intervals, or wasn't ready to eat when she was served, Julie would have to adjust accordingly. So long as Bonnie provided plenty of milk, Julie could simply fill the bottle and feed the filly. It all seemed quite uncomplicated, and Julie embarked on her duties with enthusiasm. She brought a cot and an alarm clock down from the cottage and began a rigorous routine of catnaps and filly-feeding. Her work with the two-year-olds was temporarily suspended (the exercise boys and girls dividing her mounts among themselves willingly) and, as she put it, she became a permanent resident of Stall One-and-a-Half in the West Wing of the brood-mare barn.

The colt was frolicsome and mischievous, though an inner sense warned him to be inquisitive but gentle where his little sister was concerned. Bonnie reinforced this instinct of his, permitting no roughhousing around the filly, and would swiftly nip his shoulder or flank if she thought his games were coming too close to tiring her daughter.

After two long weeks, the little filly was gaining slowly, and though she never managed to stay up for any length of time, she had learned to get herself to her hoofs and to lie down safely without being helped. She recognized Julie on sight, and was quick to shout in her thin little voice if she fancied that a meal was unduly delayed.

A third week passed, and the grueling routine was telling on Julie. She never complained, aloud or to herself, but the dark hollows under her eyes and the indoor pallor were proof enough.

The filly could now stand and move about the stall on her own; but she would not attempt to nurse. She thought that Julie was her mother and Bonnie her aunt, as Stash said; and was content to drink from the bottle, and now and then to sample a few blades of hay. Leon, Stash, Doc, and Monty on the two occasions when he zipped in and out, all suggested that Julie leave the frail little beast to her own devices, that she'd soon learn to nurse on her own. But the girl was afraid that her baby would never learn, wouldn't eat enough on her own, would give up the small ghost before she discovered how to do it—so she simply kept feeding her. It was obvious that this could not go on indefinitely, and various plans were proposed and discarded as the men tried to find a way to get the girl to back off and give the foal a chance to go on her own.

In the end, it was Stash who came up with the answer, drawing on his prodigious experience with home remedies and ancient tricks. He talked to Julie for an hour before he persuaded her, for she feared that some obscure harm would come to her baby from the attempt.

"No sir! You never heard of anybody dyin' from fresh mint leaves, now did you?" He produced a handful. "Rub 'em on your hands, then on the bottle and the nipple you use to feed her. Then catch the little princess long enough to rub some around her nose before you feed her. I don't expect her to enjoy it to start with," said Stash, "but as good as she's been eatin', I'm hopeful that her stomach's gonna win out over her nose."

"But how's that going to inspire her to nurse?" Julie shook her head. "More likely to put her off her feed, isn't it?"

"You ever know old Stash to make a horse sick? The *mint* won't make her nurse," he said patiently. "What we want is to get her used to the scent of mint when she's feedin'. Then, when she's good and certain that 'mint' means 'food' we'll rub big Bonnie's tummy and teats with mint, and stand back and hope that the princess' sense of smell finishes the job."

"We-ell, I suppose we can try it," said Julie dubiously. "But if she won't take her bottle with the smell of mint—"

"That's why you're gonna rub it on her nose first. Then she won't be able to tell the difference between what's on her nose and what's on the bottle."

"Makes sense," agreed Julie, more enthusiastically than she really felt.

But despite her misgivings, the filly had no qualms about adapting to the minted bottle. Obviously it was hers; she'd seen it hundreds of times in Julie's hand. What if there was a brand-new odor in her nose when feeding time came? Everything seemed to smell different these days. Julie had invented a game of rub-your-nose-with-mint, and since Julie wafted off gusts of mint too, what was wrong with that? Bonnie may have thought that both Julie and baby had lost their minds, and the colt shied away from the whole mint routine, but that was all right with the filly too. Julie was her mother, wasn't she?

On the morning of the third day thereafter, Bonnie stood with resignation and allowed herself to be anointed with mint. Leon held the colt off to one side, lest he register such dismay at his aromatic mother that the filly would be frightened away permanently.

Julie entered the stall, carrying the bottle as always, but instead of offering it to her baby she began a game, a sort of tag around Sunbonnet. When the filly was in a position from which she could nurse if she were inclined to do so, Julie, on the other side of the mare, reached under the bay's belly and offered the bottle. Once her tiny foal caught the notion of reaching underneath Bonnie to feed, Julie teased her along with the bottle until the filly accidentally hit one of Bonnie's nipples.

Julie could almost see the vague thoughts go through the young brain. Not a bottle, but the right size and shape . . . smells minty, as all my food does these days . . . Tentatively the little creature took hold, and when she discovered that it gave milk too, just as her bottle did, she began to nurse like an old hand at the business.

Julie eased away from them both. Either the baby did not at first realize she was gone, or else, and better yet, didn't care.

There came a worrisome moment when the foal stopped and stared around vacantly. Was she confused? Would she know how to go at it again? But the filly was not deficient in brains; had she been physically able to nurse normally, she'd have done it long before this. She was only resting. Now, like a connoisseur who had at last found precisely the thing she'd always sought after, she zeroed in again and began to drink with gusto.

That was that. Julie ducked out of the stall, ran into the sunshine, and gave a whoop of victory. Much as she doted on the filly, playing mother had been a grueling experience, and now the half-hour round-the-clock feedings were done! Besides, and more important to Julie, nature's way must be followed as closely and soon as possible, and the quicker the filly foal was on her own with Bonnie, the better it would be for her. That filly must grow up strong and healthy, and this had been the first step.

At supper, the question of names was brought up for the first time; it seemed that the whole farm had been holding its collective breath till this moment, unsure whether there would be two names to think of or, sadly, only one.

Leon said judiciously, "Out of Sunbonnet by Scotch Tweed. That suggests something on the head, made out of checkered wool, doesn't it? What was that thing your Mr. Holmes wore, Stash, with the multiple peaks?"

"That was known as a deerstalker," said Stash. "Which is not a bad name. Let's have the book down, Mr. Mc-Chrystal, you're nearest to it." He scanned the pages of the book of names that were in use or that couldn't be used again because they'd belonged to the great horses, sacred to the Jockey Club. " 'Deerstalker' seems in the clear. How's that for one?"

"I like it," said Julie. "For the colt. It's too masculine for my delicate little girl. What about 'Tam' for her?"

"Too short for a proper name, but 'Highland Tam' might be all right." Stash checked again. "Okay, Julie?"

"I could call her Tammy for a stable name."

" 'Tam' seems better to me. Too many Tammies these days."

"Okay. Tam and Deer, that's not bad at all."

There was general agreement, and Leon solemnly wrote down the names in his notebook.

"Well," said Julie, rubbing her eyes sleepily, "that's two big hurdles in one day, getting one off the bottle and naming both. I'm going to bed!"

Chapter 6

Julie leaned lazily against the paddock fence, watching the mare and the twins. It pleased her to see the little filly entering into the endless games of tag, follow-the-leader, catch-me-if-you-can, or whatever it is that foals play. Obviously the filly would never attain the size or stature of her brother, but she had lost the frail, almost transparent quality with which she'd been born. Oddly, she was more agile than her larger brother, and sometimes would trick him into coming a cropper as he twisted and turned in pursuit of her. She still tired more easily and spent more hours sleeping than young Deerstalker did, but the warm sun and spring grass were working their miracles of growth, and both Tam and Deer were doing splendidly.

Julie scaled the fence and dropped lightly on the inside. "Bonnie, did you think I'd forgotten? Gumdrop time—and I picked out all the green ones." She fished in her bulging pockets and produced an assortment of candy, carrots, and sugar cubes. The mare snuffled up the treats daintily and rubbed her head against Julie's shoulder, which show of affection Julie returned with a hug and a kiss on the end of the velvet muzzle. "Oh, Bonnie, I still do love you best of anyone!"

"Hail, horsewoman!" said a tantalizingly familiar, masculine voice behind her. She spun round, feeling herself blush. She couldn't have said why it embarrassed her to be caught hugging her horse, but she found herself stammering a reply under the friendly gaze of handsome Dirk Markham.

"Oh! Ah, err, hello, Dirk, I was just, that is, I was only, oh, ah, I was . . . hugging Bonnie," she got out.

"Who deserves it if anyone ever did. I'm glad to see that the great girl hasn't been forgotten in all the fuss that must be erupting over the twins. How old are they now?"

"Bonnie will always come first," said Julie emphatically, "and the little ones are seven weeks and four days old today. They're doing marvelously. Leon says that next week they'll be able to go out with the other mares and foals, and that little Tam, that's the filly, will be strong enough to play with the others and not get hurt. Aren't they precious?"

"They are. I heard you had a few bad days over the filly. Well, that's plainly over!" Then, with a mock gesture of formality, he bowed and said, "I'm happy to say that I'm the bearer of good news myself, Julie. Our schooling ring and barn are finished. The jumps turned out exceptionally well, and now we can build everything from a baby hunter course to an international-type Grand Prix course, complete with liverpool. Will you come over to see it all?"

"I certainly will!"

"And there's more. The hounds are settled in, and I've bought myself another horse, with whom I think I may have bitten off more than I can chew comfortably."

"Why?" After all she'd heard of Dirk's reputation and expertise with horses (from Lisa Marsden, of course), she couldn't imagine what sort of animal could make him doubtful in that fashion.

"He's a rogue. One of the finest horses I've ever set eye on, but a smart, calculating, conniving, ornery cuss of a rogue!"

"How old? And how'd he get such a reputation?" demanded the girl.

"He's five. And all his troubles, which have been plenty, stem from the area that lies between his left and right ears. He's won six races and never started for a claiming tag. His overall earnings are more than $150,000 but he's *had* it with racing, he's decided—and once he's made up his mind, everyone assures me nobody can change it."

Dirk plucked a stem of grass and began to chew it. He reminded Julie of a younger Paul Newman playing a gentleman-farmer. "He was ruled off in New York about a year ago for bolting in the Carleton Stake. The trainer had the sense to realize that the whole racetrack routine was bugging the horse, so he sent him home to the farm for six or eight months. Then, when they tried to have him reinstated, he went right back to his old tricks. He's beautifully bred, and he really can run, so if he hadn't taken a permanent dislike to everything 'racetrack' I wouldn't own him now."

"How'd he get himself permanently ruled off?" She knew that it had to be pretty bad.

"To begin with, after bolting in the Carleton and carrying the favorite and two others to the outside rail with him, he was fractious in the gate at his next start. Delayed the start for over ten minutes, so the trainer was told that he'd have to be okayed out of the gate before he could start again. When they took him to get another card, he really came unglued. He has no inhibitions about rearing any time or place, and he flipped himself over backwards just to open the act. After that he marched into the box, and threw a real fit. He leaped and reared as much as anything that big could in such a small space, and then hurled himself down and tried to crawl out under the doors."

"Sounds like a comedy," said Julie, "except that his rider could have been murdered!"

"The exercise boy who was on him was athletic enough to escape. That's when they sent the horse home the second time. When he came back again, it was just as though he'd never been away. He needed a six-months gate card, since he'd been away so long, so as soon as possible they gave him a return engagement with the starters and the gate crew. He didn't disappoint them, and put on another wild show. Then he went to propping and wheeling when he was supposed to be galloping in the mornings, and after that to refusing to set hoof on the track at all. After that, he began to scheme."

"Scheme? How?"

"For three days he seemed to have reformed. He walked out to the track peaceably, galloped properly, and everyone thought he'd recovered from whatever'd been bothering him. No such luck. He began to shed riders like autumn leaves. Some days he'd mince out onto the track and throw the jock halfway around it; others, he'd drop the boy somewhere between the shed row and the track, and go running loose all over the stable area.

"Now anybody can fall off a horse occasionally, and not get upset about it. But when day in and day out for three weeks the same horse is loose on the grounds or track, running into people and horses while another rider climbs painfully to his feet behind him, that horse establishes the bad name he's been trying to make for himself.

"They started ponying him in the mornings, and mist wouldn't melt in his mouth. Waiting for his chance. *Scheming.* They got him fit enough ponying so they could run him if he'd behave in the gate. He got his card in one start and was entered about a week afterward.

"Race day he was still on good behavior. Paddock, post parade, into the gate without a fuss. Broke on top, opened a five-length lead down the backside, and then he was holding all the cards. He simply never—made—the—turn!"

"What!"

"That's right. He bolted straight to the outside rail, but this time he tried to jump it. Made it, too, except that he stumbled badly when he landed . . . in the parking lot! There weren't any cars where he came down, luckily, and the jock fell clear of him, with a cracked arm and collarbone but glad to be alive.

"Why the nag wasn't damaged or killed is a mystery, but that's why he was ruled off for life, and why I have him now."

"Some story," said the girl, a little breathless. "What will you do if he doesn't want to be a show horse either? He acts according to his own whims, I'd say, with a vengeance."

"He does. I really haven't thought that far ahead, Julie," said Dirk, gazing at her with those almost hypnotic blue eyes. "Selling him again, if that mental attitude persists, is out of the question. He'd be bound to hurt someone eventually. That would mean I'd be stuck with him. But I have a hunch that he could be one of the world's great jumpers—*if* I can find the key to him, the map of his brains. If I can make him *like* to jump, truly enjoy it, then I doubt there's any fence he wouldn't try, just for the pleasure of it."

Julie tried to imagine the horse. "What's he look like?" she asked finally.

"Sixteen three, dark bay or brown, four white stockings and a stripe and snip," Dirk reeled off easily.

"Good grief, you're asking for it, aren't you?" Seeing his puzzled look, she chanted:

> One white foot, buy him;
> Two white feet, try him;
> Three white feet, doubt him;
> Four white, do without him!

Dirk laughed. "See what you mean. A rather silly old superstition, isn't it?"

"Well, if you really want to be absurd, there's a variation on the theme that says, 'Four white feet and a long white nose, knock him on the head and feed him to the crows!'"

"I hope it won't come to that," said Dirk.

"Who's being fed to the crows, may I ask?" It was Leon Pitt, on his way to the mare fields to begin bringing them in to feed and do up for the night.

"Oh, Leon, is it that time already? I lost track of hours," said Julie with rue. "Have you met Dirk Markham?"

"Twice, and this is three. How are you, Mr. Markham?" He solemnly shook hands. "Day you brought him and his sister to see the farm, before the twins were born, and then how do you s'pose he knew where to find you today?"

"How silly of me," said Julie, flustered for no evident reason. "And I forgot all about the time when Alexis came too."

Leon smiled at her discomfort . . . he'd exchanged a few words with Dirk Markham, and thus far he liked him very well. Leon's opinion was that there were two kinds of people, animal people and non-animal people. The former had a certain outgoing quality, an openness about them that he believed to be the reason why dogs and horses and any number of other beasts great and small were drawn to them. The latter were rarely found in Leon's world, but when they were, he steered shy of them. It was his only prejudice.

"Can I help with something?" Dirk asked now.

"Sure can," said Leon, handing him a lead shank. "Nat's here afternoons to help do up, but he's at the dentist today and Julie and I have lots to finish. Have thirty-four mares and twenty-six—no, almost forgot the twosome— that's twenty-seven foals to bring in."

The two men headed down the lane, and Julie stood smiling after them. She opened the gate and called her mare. As her little foursome made its way up to the barn, she said to Bonnie (who was, after all, her best friend), "Leon seems to have changed his mind about spooky old Croydon Farm, or he wouldn't even let Dirk on Fieldstone."

They were in the middle of feeding when Stash thrust his head inside the door. "Hi there, Julie."

"Hey Stash! You remember Dirk Markham? The new master at Croydon?"

"Mr. Markham, nice to see you again."

Julie wondered: had she really detected a tone of dubiousness in that familiar voice, or had she imagined it? Stash grabbed the hose and began watering, while Julie and Leon finished doling out portions of grain. Dirk was brooming the floor. As they worked along in the common bond of stable chores, Julie directed a steady flow of questions at Dirk on the progress of renovating Croydon.

"The jumper ring's already finished," she informed Stash, "and they can build everything from baby hunter fences to a Grand Prix course complete with liverpool."

"Fascinatin'. Who hunts babies, though, and what on earth is a liverpool? A pond to bathe your liver in?"

"It's a, well, it's a jump with a, uh—" she laughed and ended with, "I don't know. What is a liverpool, Dirk?"

"A type of open jumper or steeplechase obstacle, comprised of a hedge with or without rails over or behind it, and a ditch filled with water in front. Put that all together and you have a pretty wide-spread fence. If a show horse puts a hoof in the water, he's penalized with faults just as if he'd knocked down a rail."

"And I'll have you both know that I have been invited to see that course, liverpool and all," said Julie to her friends.

"Invitation's open for anyone who cares to come," said Dirk. "We'll have an open house when everything's finished, but since the horses are most important to Lex and me, we began with their accommodations and left the house for last. The ring's done, we've fenced two small paddocks for immediate use, and the barn's about ready."

"When your horses comin'?"

"In a day or two, as soon as the barn's had its last touch. I think Croydon's going to be a lucky place for me," said Dirk, watching Julie. "It already has once—"

"When?" asked Julie, responding innocently to the obvious setup.

"When I found you and a welcome basket on my front porch."

"Oh." For the third time that afternoon, Julie found herself feeling strange and awkward, the color flooding her cheeks as though she were thirteen again and mooning over Monty Everett. It wasn't her custom to fish for compliments, and while she was secure in all her relationships with the population of Fieldstone, it was hardly the type of situation in which compliments are flung casually about. Thus, when flattery was thrown at her, she was hopelessly inept at fielding it.

Stash caught Leon's eye, and they exchanged a long look. Dirk said, "By the way, I have another invitation for a Fieldstone resident."

"Someone else?" Julie was puzzled. Leon stepped backwards with a bemused look, waiting to see what was coming. Stash began coiling the hose, and he wasn't about to miss a thing either.

"Cache," said Dirk. "An invitation to a stay at Croydon, if you'd like to bring him. You'd be doing me a big favor. Lex is away most of the time between now and the middle of November, and with my new horse's reputation, I'd like to have someone around when I work with him. In return, I'd help you with Cache. Besides," he said, explaining a little too much, thought Stash, "it's always more fun schooling greenies when there's someone with you to appreciate your progress."

"Oh wow," said Julie, "Cache accepts with pleasure! What a super idea!" She looked at Leon and Stash, obviously expecting a comment.

"Sounds fine," said Leon.

"Uh-oh!" said Stash.

"Uh-oh?" said Julie, uncertain that she'd heard him rightly. "What do you mean, uh-oh?"

Stash hadn't meant to be heard at all, but being caught, made a gallant effort to wriggle off his hook. "Uh-oh, looks like the hose is springin' a leak," he exclaimed, fumbling with the remaining section of hose. Unable to locate a drop of water, he briskly added, "And I told Pop I'd meet him at the stallion barn at five and I'm late!"

Julie looked at her watch. "Four minutes late, and we all know how unreasonable Pop can be."

"Hate to be late," mumbled Stash, heading for the stable door.

"What's the matter with him?" demanded Julie.

"Maybe he's afraid you won't have time for the yearlings if you take Cache to Croydon," suggested Leon, knowing perfectly well what was on Stash's mind.

"He knows better than that," Julie snapped. "I start work at five, finish about eleven, which means I can be at Croydon by eleven-thirty. Allow half an hour to dust him off and catch his stall, that's only noon. Then if I ride him for an hour, that's one o'clock. Another hour to cool him out and do him up, and that's only two P.M. I can certainly be back here by two-thirty. That still gives me an hour with the yearlings before Bonnie begins looking for me. Then I come here, play with her and the twins, and help you do up."

Dirk listened quietly through this entire recital, and when he was sure she'd finished, said, "What about lunch?"

"Oh! Well, I've been getting a little hippy lately, and I've been meaning to go on a diet. . . ."

At the sheer lunacy of this, Leon gave a shout of merriment. Even Julie had to grin, for the truth was that no matter how often she answered her appetite alarm, the scale never registered more than a hundred and five.

"We'll manage some watercress sandwiches and clover tea at Croydon especially for you," Dirk promised. "I'll come over for Cache, with a van, tomorrow at noon. All right?"

"Right," said Julie.

And although Stash was far away, Leon could have sworn he heard the ghostly echo of the groom's voice saying *Uh-oh.* . . .

Chapter 7

"There he is," said Dirk, allowing his hand to rest in a brotherly way on Julie's shoulder. They looked into the stall together.

"What's his name?" Julie asked; it was insulting to refer to an animal by anything but its given name.

"His registered name is Not A Clue. Which is fitting enough, since he's by Puzzled out of a mare called Lost In Thought. But I don't care who he's been or what he's done, and because he's beginning a new life with me, I thought I'd start him out fresh with a new name. Soul-searching."

"Soul-searching. Yes. I like that better. It has a ring. And Not A Clue sounds too dubious, as if you hadn't any idea why he does what he does."

"Which I don't, but there's no sense belaboring that subject. If you like Soul-searching, I'll keep it for certain," said Dirk, as he led the big brown horse from the stall for Julie's further inspection. Soul-searching was impressive enough; Julie agreed with Dirk that here was one of the most beautifully constructed beasts she'd ever seen. There might be technical flaws in his conformation, but she could see not a one. With a silent apology to Bonnie, who was somewhat bent out of shape due to her recent pregnancy, Julie praised the horse with enthusiasm and congratulated Dirk on his find.

"Come out to the paddock," said Dirk. "I'll turn him loose so that you can see him move. Don't be afraid, his cussedness doesn't extend to biting."

"I can tell that from his eyes," said Julie.

They watched him walk briskly around the fence to stretch his legs, then trot and canter. "I don't know much

71

about what makes a jumper," the girl said, "but I've seen enough horses to know that this one has more athletic ability than most any I've come across, except maybe Cache. Why, he has springs instead of shoes! I'll bet he can do anything he pleases; if only what you want him to do pleases him, you're in business." She turned to look up at Dirk. "I'm sure you'll fix him, I *know* it. There's an answer to everything about horses if you can find it."

Dirk smiled at her earnest tone. "I'll keep looking till I do. Let's leave the old boy here a while. Let me show you the kennels and hounds."

"Oh, yes!"

The big kennel ran directly north-to-south, a wooden building that they entered from outside through an ordinary door with a white china knob. Within, there were rugs and mats for the hounds, and in a moment there were also hounds, definitely not lying down, but leaping and begging and whimpering with joy. "Down, gentlemen," said Dirk calmly, and they obeyed at once. "We'll go out and view the run," he said to Julie.

On the eastern side of the kennel was a large, anchor-fenced area, which Julie noted had been thoughtfully laid out around a huge oak tree so that there was always shade for the dogs, another sign of Dirk Markham's affection for animals. There was a gate set into its southern side, fastened with a peculiar-looking drop-latch. In the east wall had been cut five dog-sized entrances which the hounds, excited by the human company, kept dashing into and out from; these were protected by wooden canopies so that wind and weather would not penetrate the indoor quarters.

"The hounds remind me," said Dirk as they walked back to look once more at Soul-searching, "pretty-soon I'd like to take you up on that promise to introduce me to the local farmers, or landowners if they don't farm. I want permission to hunt over their acreage."

"Any day I have the time, Dirk."

"Of course, I'll assume all responsibility for their fence lines and crops and, well, everything. I want to get their consent, too, to panel the countryside."

"That's nice," said Julie with a straight face. "Wormy chestnut or redwood? Then you'll hang pipes and escutcheons on the panels, naturally, and maybe crossed sabers, and put in a very large fireplace, about seven hundred yards high; and you'll have the biggest den in the state. What's 'panel' mean?"

He threw back his head and laughed. "The reasons for paneling are as follows: One, most fences that are built to contain horses are too high to jump, and hunting isn't meant to be a strain on horse or rider, whatever horror stories you've heard—at least, not *my* hunt. I want to watch the hounds at work and give my mount a pleasant hour or two of exercise. Two, I wouldn't want to damage any other man's gates and fences, so I'd prefer to build and maintain my own panels within the existing fence lines. So three, the panels would be made of solid, jumpable materials—telephone poles cut to size, stone walls, coops (which are triangular and made of wood), that sort of thing. They lessen the probability of accidents."

"Panels are really hurdles, then."

"That's right. And I doubt that we'll find much opposition to them in this part of the world, because most of the landowners hereabouts will be riding with the hunt anyway."

"It sounds like an English movie already," said Julie irrepressibly. "All we need is a murder and a policeman from—oh, I'm sorry, I never thought."

She could not be sure that a shadow had crossed his face and was gone. He said lightly, "Never mind that old tale, we're not haunted here at Croydon," with emphasis on the name, as though he were defying ghosts.

But the phantom of a creepy feeling stayed with Julie almost halfway home to Fieldstone Farm.

"Sounds great," said Leon when Julie told them of the fox-hunt plans. Stash made a noncommittal noise. When the girl had gone on to see Bonnie, Leon said to his old friend, "I know why you're gruffin' around like that, don't think you got me fooled."

"Never intended to fool you. Just don't want to influence Julie. But I got my loyalties and preferences, and one of 'em is Monty Everett, who I worked for his father many and many a year back home," said Stash moodily.

"If he never says anything to Julie, he's got to expect competition to move in. She's not gettin' any younger."

"Poor old lady," said Stash. "Spinster, moldin' on the vine. I don't mind this Markham so much, but he keeps cuttin' in when Monty's away."

"Monty's *always* away. Dirk doesn't know anything about those two, after all. Fact is, Julie herself doesn't know about 'em, except that Monty's her boss and she works for him."

"Julie's not so dense as all that, Leon."

"No, but I don't see any big diamond shiny and elegant on her finger, either. Let Monty stand up for his own rights, and don't be sayin' *uh-oh* every whipstitch."

"You're on Markham's side," accused Stash, shaking a long lean finger under Leon's nose. "*Uh-oh!* How you like them apples?"

"They're sour," said Leon.

It was more than a week later when Monty did arrive home for a relaxing brief vacation, only to find Julie spending every spare minute schooling Cache at Croydon, walking fence lines, watching panels go up, playing with Bonnie's twins. . . . "I'd really love to run over to Deepwater and look at that mare with you, Monty dear, but Bonnie expects me this time every day and Dirk's putting up an aiken and I promised to help gather brush and I couldn't disappoint her and go back on my solemn pledged word to him, now could I?" . . . Monty stuck it out for three days and then, more weary and frazzled than when he'd appeared, left abruptly for New York to see a man about a horse in Florida, or so he snapped out as he left. Stash frowned, stared at Leon, shook his head.

"Afraid Monty left the words until just too late. Afraid he'll never get 'em out now, with big handsome Duck in control."

"Dirk, you nonesuch!"

"I know it. Just feel bad. Things aren't headin' for

much joy around this place. Wish I'da stayed at St. Clair and groomed racehorses," grunted Stash, half meaning it. "Wouldn't have seen the hope of my life go gurglin' down the drain. And to a man that lives in a haunted house."

"Now you cut that out, Stash Watkins! That's too serious a subject to take lightly," said Leon with ferocity.

"Every time Julie goes over there, I expect her back with something awful trailin' her. You forget about that glass axe?" persisted Stash.

"No. I keep studying it, every time I see that bit of a limp still on Pushy. Who did it? That frets me."

"Me too. Let's go feed mares, son."

"I'm with you, daddy," said Leon.

At Croydon, the house was only beginning to be renovated and made livable. The barn and kennels had been for the important people, Dirk told Julie in her own fashion; the house was just for a couple of human beings. Alexis had been away for three weeks now, and would be on the New York and Connecticut circuits for two more. She had three horses with her; however, she was dropping by their home shortly to leave one horse to rest and pick up another which had been freshened at the farm. She would only be there overnight, said Dirk, sighing a little. "You two have hardly *met,* have you? She's off riding at odd hours or out of town at the shows. I wish you could get to know each other, you're both grand girls."

Julie, who was gradually getting used to this sort of praise from the young man, said, "She's the prettiest girl I ever met around here, Dirk. Your parents must have been beautiful."

He smiled and said, "Look in your mirror for an even prettier girl, Julie," and began talking about the horse that Lex was bringing home. "Castle Creek's his name, and she shows him in the amateur/owner jumper division, where participants are restricted to horses that are owned and ridden by amateurs only. Creek's done well this season; he won several big classes, which means he's had to jump a lot more fences than a horse of lesser ability."

"Why?"

"In the jumper division, the horses go the first round. Then all horses who've gone clean—that is to say, without incurring faults—or those with an equal number of faults if no horse goes clean, jump off over a raised course."

"In case of no clean horses, they jump the same course again, don't they?"

"Yes, they won't raise the fences if nobody got around clean the first time. Say, am I instructing you about a topic you already have down pat? I lose track of what I've told you."

"No, every time I learn something new."

"Good. You're a great pupil. At any rate, this system of raising the fences or jumping the same course again goes on until one winner emerges. In some cases, the second or third jump-off is decided by the clock; that means that the horse with no faults or the least number of 'em, plus the fastest time, wins. And since it would be unusual, to put it mildly, for two horses to have the same split-second timing, it's an effectual way of breaking an interminable tie.

"Castle Creek is fantastic. He winds up in many jump-offs, and Lex has decided that he needs some rest. She's bringing him home to exchange him for her second-year green working hunter, On Target, whom you met yesterday. He's been resting at home since he made a clean sweep of the championships of all three shows that make up the Florida circuit in February and. March."

"Green" means that a horse is in its first or second year of showing. Dirk went on: "He was shown lightly last year and did well, but since he was only three years old then, Lex didn't campaign him very hard. This year he's really come to himself, and did marvelously in Florida."

"He'd be jumping obstacles at three-feet-nine high, wouldn't he?"

"That's good homework. Yes, first-year division means three-feet-six, then next year they put them up three inches. Working hunters, like any other hunters, are shown over courses with obstacles that simulate those found in hunt country, just like the ones we've been putting up: stone walls, post-and-rail, chicken coops, aikens, all kinds of gates—"

"What kinds? Tell me!"

"Fairfield gates, garden gates, white gates, Toronto banks . . . those are false aiken shapes made of wood and painted to look like a natural aiken, mottled green and brown, as if it were actually a rail fence with a huge pile of brush in front, instead of a quarter-round of wood. You'll see some of them soon, I think."

"Where?"

He winked. "At the horse show we're all going to in September."

"That's literally *months* away!"

"Too much work before that to get away. Also, a few hunts. But we'll all go up to the Huntington Valley show in the autumn and watch Lex perform."

"Monty too?" asked Julie with a start of near-forgotten loyalty.

"If he can get away from the track, sure."

Julie gazed away thoughtfully, and found herself staring at the house, which looked as spectral as ever. It had yet to be painted. "Dirk—"

"What?"

"Are there such things as ghosts?"

"Only in minds," he said cryptically. "While we're on the topic, I forgot to mention the herringbone, which is simply a rectangle with herringbone-style crosspieces in it."

"That's a ghost?"

"That's an obstacle. Hunters are judged," he went on in a pedantic and don't-change-my-subject tone, "on performance, which is their form, how they took each fence; on manners, the way in which they went about it—that is, did they misbehave and buck, were they sulky or cheerful, did the rider have an easy trip or work hard all the way; and on way of going, which refers to what sort of mover the animal is—does he move close to the ground, with the floating illusion of a 'daisy cutter,' or does he break a lot of knee and look choppy, which indicates a bad mover.

"Things like chipping in—getting too close to a fence

before takeoff—or leaving out a stride—taking off from too far away—or hanging a leg—which is very dangerous —are penalized heavily. Usually one such fence will throw you right out of the ribbons, since the whole idea is to present an even, fluid picture that just flows consistently from fence to fence."

"That sounds lovely," said Julie.

Why did he avoid the subject of ghosts?

"There are no jump-offs with hunters," he continued. "They make it strictly on the judges' preferences and decision, so you can see what it means when Lex pleases many different judges, all of whom consistently rate her horse as best, or at least put him in the top four in class after class. Working hunters are judged solely on performance, of course, and conformation or 'strip' hunters are rated first on their performance over fences, then according to their physical structure and beauty. So unless you have a fine-looking hunter, you can be called out first on performance and then moved back to second or third on looks, and *therefore,*" he said, holding up a finger and looking like a professor, "with a homely horse, you stay in the working division, where performance alone earns you the ribbon and the accompanying silver plate or check."

"So isn't On Target pretty enough?"

"Not quite. But top-notch for a working hunter."

"What about Castle Creek?"

"You're bouncing from hunters to jumpers, you know."

"*I* know. I just thought, he must be gorgeous; he is in the biggest division, isn't he?"

"That's right. Can you tick me off the divisions of jumpers?"

"Like the multiplication table," said Julie, and proceeded with a rush. "There are three, governed by how much money a horse has won. Preliminary starts him off, then after he's earned so much, he goes into intermediate, with higher and tougher fences; when he earns his way out of that, he competes in the biggest division, the open, which has the very highest fences and the hardest courses of all. Those fences go what, four-feet-six to five feet?"

"And up to seven feet or even more."

"The jumper's scored mathematically by faults, either touching or knocking down the obstacles. There isn't any limit to the types of fences and sometimes the stranger the better."

"Though they do try not to frighten the horses," added Dirk.

"More often than not the clock's the deciding factor," said Julie, brain working away at her mental card index. "When riders go against the clock, they make daring short cuts to fences, jump their obstacles diagonally instead of straight, make time turns—"

"Which are . . . ?"

"They turn their horses in mid-air to save time on landing. I've never seen it, just listened to you, but it sounds thrilling. Lex and Castle Creek must be super at all of that!"

"Matter of fact, she recently won a class with him in which she jumped an eleven-fence course clean four times —that's forty-four fences—before finally winning the class. That's a sight of fences to jump in a row without so much as a rub!"

As Julie looked up at the house again, he went on rapidly, really as though he meant to distract her before she could switch subjects once more. "Lex's November Witch is cleaning house too. She made a clean sweep of all the working hunter classes at Fairlawn Hunt Club two weeks ago, and when Lex is cracking with her she simply can't be beaten. Every trip she puts up is the equivalent of a 'stake round' of old, in which the mare really runs and jumps—has a fast pace, I mean, and jumps all her fences high and handsome."

"I want to see her in action!"

"You will, often. Not to brag, but she's sort of creating a small revolution in the hunter division."

"How?"

"With so many people showing their horses on illegal tranquilizers, there was a time when all you'd see in the hunter division was horses ditty-bopping around the course, taking tiny strides and going very slowly. Lex on Witch, with her strong pace and bold way of jumping, was noticeably out of place. But then, one old and respected judge began defying the arbitrary pinning of these slowpokes, saying that no real hunter ever went so slowly, and what was the division coming to? He started to pin Lex over the others, saying in print that you either had to rank Alexis Markham above all the others or below them, but you could hardly rate her type of trip alongside theirs! That was last year. Now a lot of other judges have followed suit, and so long as Lex gets her eight brilliant fences, she wins. And some people have started taking their hunters off tranquilizers and really riding them again.

"Lex has a natural eye and fantastic timing—she can see a distance from miles away as it were—which is by way of saying that she can judge the approaches and take-offs of her fences with absolute accuracy. And she—"

"Well, what about *your* showing?" asked Julie, as Dirk seemed to be winding up to go on all day about his sister.

"Croydon will take all my time till fall, but then I'm planning to make the indoor circuit, starting with Spectrum in Philly, the last week in September; on to Pennsylvania National at Harrisburg, Washington International in D.C., the National Horse Show at Madison Square Garden, and if my horses are still in good shape, on to the final one of the season, the Royal Winter Fair in Toronto, last week in November."

"Good, then you'll be here at Croydon all summer," said Julie happily.

"Does that please you?"

"Of course! Think how much I'd miss Soul-searching, and what would Cache do with my amateur whacks at schooling him?" She looked at her watch. "Gosh, I've got to run."

"How long have you been coming here to Croydon now?" asked Dirk, catching her wrist gently to keep her from whirling away.

"Let's see. We brought Cache over when the twins were seven weeks and five days old. Nine days later Monty came home for three days. Lex left two days later and she's been gone just three weeks today. That's, umm, oh, nuts . . . well, the twins are twelve weeks and five days old as of this morning, minus seven weeks five days leaves oh let me see ah you can't do this in your head oh great day in the afternoon I'll never get it oh," said Julie, somehow coming up after this spate with the right total, "it's five weeks."

"And in all that time I don't believe I ever got around to telling you that I think you're the grandest girl in the whole universe," said Dirk, looking into her eyes. "But I do, you know."

"Thank you. I'm pretty fond of you too," said Julie, hearing her own voice smack flat and without expression and wondering why it should do that.

"I'm rather certain, Miss Jefferson, that I am in love with you."

"I'm quite certain, Mr. Markham, that we'd better not mention the subject again until I've thought it out some," said Julie, a tiny catch of something like fear in her throat. The fact was that she had thought a lot of Dirk at odd times when she wasn't thinking of horses, and was completely mystified as to the state of her feelings about him.

"Then I'll swear a dark and bloody oath not to bring it up again till you do, if only to keep you from staying away from Croydon."

"How well you know me," said Julie uncomfortably.

"Yes, I think I do. Listen, will you do me a gargantuan favor? I have to be away for twenty-four hours beginning tomorrow morning. Lex isn't due here till day after tomorrow. I hate to impose, but would you feed the horses and dogs and do the light afternoon chores tomorrow for me? I can take care of the stock before I leave, and I'll leave everything dished out for supper; all you'll have to do is put it into the kennels and the barn, water them—"

"That's not a gigantic favor at all, I'd love it. Matter of fact," said Julie, grinning, "I can bring Pushy and Nana over to introduce them around, and if Nana commits any atrocities, I can repair them before you get back!"

"Hey, thanks. They'll all be tided over nicely then till Lex arrives. The animals, I mean."

"No trouble at all," said Julie. "I'll get up fifteen minutes earlier and that'll give me loads of time."

"You're okay, neighbor."

"You aren't so bad yourself, neighbor," said Julie Jeferson, and took off for home.

Chapter 8

Julie finished her riding at Fieldstone early. They had already shipped four or five two-year-olds to Monty, so she had a little more time these days for herself. Too, she *had* set her alarm a quarter of an hour before, thus confusing Nana and depressing Pushy when they were shoved out into the June predawn darkness prior to their accustomed minute. Now she cleaned her tack and ran off to the yearling barn to tell Stash she'd be away longer than usual, doing up at Croydon for Dirk.

"That's nice of you," said Stash, looking as if he thought it was utterly miserable of her.

"Dirk's a wonderful teacher, so patient with me and Cache, and this is almost the first time I've had the chance to help him at all."

"Why, you help him all the time. More'n you help your old pals, seems to me."

"Like who? You? Leon?" she demanded.

"Well, no, not us," he relented.

"Monty? He's never here!"

"It was just a kind o' miserable idea I threw out without thinkin'," said Stash. "Don't mind me, Julie, my left toe's got the frostbite kickin' up again."

"The summer frostbite. It strikes with deadly swiftness on such a morning," she said in a sepulchral voice. "I don't know why you don't like Dirk, honestly, Stash! He's one of the nicest, most thoughtful, accommodating, kindest men I know. And he's real horse folks."

"And he sneaks around Monty's back, covetin' what isn't his," Stash snapped.

It was so uncharacteristic an outburst that Julie simply stared.

83

"You're Monty's girl," mumbled the groom, inspecting the toe of his shoe. "That's the way it is."

"Who ever said I was Monty's girl? We've been friends since I was a kid, but I'm not his girl! I'm my girl, and Bonnie's and the twins', and Dad's and Mr. T's and yours and Leon's too for that matter, but I'm not Monty's girl in any sense! He's never *here,*" Julie wailed; "he's never around for me to be his girl!"

"He got a job to do."

"And a mouth that he never says anything with except about racehorses! Don't you go playing Cupid, Mr. Watkins, or I'll—I'll sic Leon on you! *He* likes Dirk."

"Funny thing he does," said Stash, looking woefully up at her, " 'cause he hates that Croydon place like poison. Says it isn't a house that'll rest till the old couple's been revengified."

"And don't start talking like Stepin Fetchit to get around me, Stash," she said sternly; at ease with him now, though. "You know more English than I ever will. You tell me you'll feel better about Dirk Markham, and I'll forgive you for that Monty stuff."

"I will try to think good thoughts about Dirk Markham," stated her old friend. "His sister I'm not so sure of."

"She's strange, sort of aloof, but I think it's her youth and inexperience with people."

"Nope. She's jealous o' Dirk."

"But he's her brother!"

"Stepbrother."

"What?" she yipped.

"I been doing a little homework on the Markhams."

"A little snooping, you mean."

"I do not stoop to snoop," said Stash, looking down his nose. "I investigate interesting items. And horses. And sometimes people."

"What else did you find out?" she couldn't help asking him.

"They come from not far from here, originally. Near Cochranville, I think. Duck's—I mean, Dirk's father married Lex's mother when the girl was only six, and not very long afterwards they both caught sick and died. That left

Dirk, who was maybe seventeen, to bring up Lex by himself—no other relations, I guess—and if they hadn't had
money he couldn't have done it, but he managed to be
brother and father and mother to that little kid. This was
maybe twelve-thirteen years ago. They moved away pretty
soon, and just came back this year to the territory. So she
thinks the moon sets and the sun rises on him, and she's
jealous of you, and that's plain to anybody that sees the
three of you together, which I did once. And once to
Stash 'Mr. Holmes' Watkins is enough, Julie."

"But doesn't that make Dirk a wonderful guy, even in
your eyes? Taking on the rearing of his stepsister like
that?"

"I only thought he oughtn't to crowd in on Monty, I
told you that. He doesn't seem like too bad a fellow
otherwise," said Stash cautiously. "Good with horses, I
give him that."

"Poor girl," said Julie, musing. "I've got to get to know
her better. I'm certainly not out to take her entire family
away from her." It would probably be a hard task, considering Lex's lack of cordiality and her habit of disap-
pearing when anyone came near, but it must be done.
"Think good thoughts, Stash," she said. "It's much too
early to do up at Croydon, so I'm going in to Meriden to
the saddlery shop to buy halters for the twins. Bye!"

It was half a minute before that sank in on Stash.
"Halters?" he exclaimed to the empty barn. "Those foals
are three months old, and they won't need new halters
for another three! Julie is out of her big-blue-eyed head."

Julie merely liked to be prepared. It was true that the
weanling-size halters wouldn't be needed for quite a while,
but she wanted to give them something and could think
of nothing else that was at all practical. She chose two
fine halters, the wonderful thick smell of horse-leather all
around her, and glanced at her watch and dropped by the
supermarket for a huge bag of gumdrops for Bonnie.

She then went home again, ate lunch (which she had
been skipping for too long), and ran down to visit her
mare and the twins. She showed Bonnie the halters, which
seemed to interest the mare genuinely, almost as if she

knew what they'd be used for. "Let's try one on Deer," said Julie, and did so. "Hmm. Lot of growing to do, baby. Still, when you're that big, we'll be ready for you. Hi, Tam honey," she said as the little filly came to her side. "No use trying one on you for size, it would only embarrass you. You *are* growing, though, isn't she, Bonnie?" The filly nuzzled her with love. "You dear, dear little thing," said Julie, "to think they didn't want to raise you! You'll be the sweetest—that is, the second sweetest horse on Fieldstone, right next to your mommy!"

She took a long farewell of the three of them, rushed off to the cottage to collect Pushy and Nana, and hightailed it for Croydon, where she intended to ride Cache before doing the chores.

Cache, the big gray, no longer showed any signs of his long bout with semistarvation. She had schooled him slowly at Dirk's suggestion, gradually erasing some of his racing-days habits, though not all of them as yet. He whinnied a greeting to her as she arrived.

She led him out, saddled him, and telling both dogs to stay put, began to walk Cache. Walk and halt, walk and halt, making sure that he stopped square on all four feet, which gained him praise and patting. Then she went on to a sitting trot with many changes of direction, not planned but just as they occurred to her. Now and then she would halt again, and if he stopped squarely, there were further compliments and a sugar cube.

The sky was slowly clouding over, but as yet the clouds were white and the breeze was low; it was a lovely day, and Croydon was becoming a beautiful place. Julie started on transitions: she would trot along at a slow pace, then "close her legs around him" but not permit him to increase speed, so that he would take longer strides for a few steps, then come back to an ordinary trot. Sometimes he would be asked to shorten his stride, too, but the general idea was that whether she told him to lengthen or shorten, she was trying to get him to "listen" to her requests and to respond immediately.

This is an important part of building the foundation for a jumper—or for any sort of horse—because if the horse is approaching a fence and the rider sees, for example, that the distance is wrong and wants to make an adjustment, he must be able to lengthen or shorten the animal's stride instantly and without an argument; otherwise he will not have what is called a smooth fence.

Julie also practiced with Cache making transitions at the canter, then from trot to canter and trot to walk, canter to walk and walk to sitting trot to anything that entered her mind. She was constantly changing her directions and making Cache bend his body in the line of his turn. "It does no good," she told him kindly but firmly, "to be turning to the right if your body's bent to the left and you're just groping around with your right shoulder and foreleg in that half-hearted way!" Cache blew through his nose and tried again. He was a patient soul and longed to please her, whatever in the world she was trying to make him do.

After some sugar cubes for an especially nice try, she practiced his leads at the canter. He was a bit one-sided, favoring his left lead: this was a leftover from his race-track days. But he was growing much better about breaking his right lead. Again, more praise, more pats, more sugar.

She got him to jog over some rails that lay on the ground. Like most horses who have been at the track, Cache tended to be in a hurry about everything, and one of her biggest problems was to make him relax and slow down. Since Dirk was absent, she would not jump anything, but she did jog him over the rails while forcing him to be quiet and steady. Sometimes she would trot up to a rail and halt, then have him step over it; though she didn't do that often, for fear he would get the idea that he should always stop at an obstacle and acquire the bad habit of refusing.

The schooling went well—she thought it was his best day thus far—and she found that she had used up all her sugar. While she was cooling him out, she realized for the first time how very quiet Croydon was, and how much she had subconsciously been missing Dirk.

Suppose it had been Monty she'd been with every afternoon. Would she be missing *him* this much?

"Of course!" she said sharply to Cache, who turned his head to gaze at her inquiringly.

"Well," she said more quietly, "I really don't know."

She gave the gray a bath, scraped him off, let him nibble delicately at some grass till he was dry, brushed him, picked out his feet, and took him back to his stall, the two dogs padding behind her. She then watered and hayed all the horses in the barn, ten including Cache, and since it was still early to give them their grain, she took a squint at the darkening sky, and decided to take care of the hounds next. A storm seemed to be brewing far down on the weather side, and the breeze had freshened to a wind.

Dirk had put the food dishes and a huge glass jar of bacon drippings next to the latched gate of the run, since the dogs were fed there rather than in the sleeping quarters. All she had to do was to top the dishes with fat and set them inside the gate. But the latch resisted her for some time, till she learned the trick of opening it. She did it a few times so that she'd have it down pat for later use (*when?* asked a small voice in her head), then went in and was deluged with hounds till, imitating Dirk's calm authoritative manner, she said, "Down, gentlemen," and they backed off, hindquarters writhing eagerly. She put the dishes in a wide-spaced row and went out again, pushed the hose through the anchor fence, reentered, filled up their watering tubs with fresh drink from the hose, and went back to the stable to feed the horses their grain.

Thunder growled on the horizon.

Julie glanced involuntarily toward the big unpainted house. It stood like a glum and silent watcher on its knoll, the windows now curtained but the general air of emptiness still hanging about it. She gave a slight shiver. She wished that Dirk were here.

He was a fine caretaker of his animals, for where the hounds had had bacon drippings, in the stable carrots topped off each horse's feed ration. He obviously loved them in the way that Julie loved all beasts. She glanced down at Nana, still at her heels, and assumed that Pushy

was not far behind. She fed the horses, said good-night
to her Cache, and hooked the big chains across the ends
of the barn; these hung there in case a horse should somehow get loose during the night, for since it was summer,
the doors at either end were left open for better circulation of air, and the chains were a simple device for keeping in would-be truants.

As she turned from the barn, Julie was appalled to see
Nana prick up what she could of her ears, give a preliminary wiggle, and bolt off at full throttle and in full
cry toward the house.

"Beagle!" she screamed after the brute. "Nana, you
come *back* here!" She gave a piercing whistle, which Stash
had taught to her a dozen years before; but of course
Nana never ever heard anything when she was excited, or
obeyed an order if there was some item of interest Out
There that only she could detect. Julie set out after her
at a run.

The thunder was a lot nearer by now.

Halfway between the barn and the house, she was
abruptly surrounded and overrun by ten couple of hounds,
loping and baying and affectionately inundating her with
their long spotted bodies in order to lick her face. Julie,
so startled as to be unnerved, let out a shriek. The dogs
backed away, puzzled. Julie wailed.

"How—where—who—OH!" She grasped one by the
loose skin of his nape and after a couple of strenuous
tries, caught a second. Two at a time were all she could
hold, and the others, all eighteen of them, were going into
something that resembled a witches' dance on Halloween
night, the effect enhanced by the dark sky and lowering
rack of cloud. Baying and barks mingled with a crack of
thunder.

How did you call hunting hounds? She struggled to
remember, as the hounds in turn struggled to get out of
her grip. "Yoicks?" she shouted tentatively. "Yoicks,
fellas?" Nothing. "Tantivy, tally-ho, loo wind 'em?" she
tried, remembering vaguely a couple of British movies.
Nothing.

She set off toward the kennels, dragging the two with

her. "Here boys, come on pups, come on!" A few of them
followed her inquisitively, the others began to quest and
romp. She made the kennel and shoved them into the run,
slammed the gate and started back for the rest of the pack.
The two she thought she had just locked up flew past her
on their way to join the gang again. Julie stopped dead
and gaped. How could this *be*?

She caught one more and, he being a wriggly one, hoisted
him into her arms and carried him to the kennel. The gate
was closed and latched. She stood there, holding the dog
in a ridiculous upside-down pose, trying to remember.
Hadn't this door been closed and latched a minute ago,
when she'd brought the first pair? She wasn't certain. She
threw in the writhing hound and definitely locked the door.
He caught up with her in less than a quarter of a minute
and pirouetted around her, bugling with the fun of it. She
fell on him and got him over her shoulder and marched
back to the run. The gate was indeed closed. How had
the wretched hound. . . . Then she recollected the door in
the north end of the wooden building that served the animals for shelter at night or in uncomfortable weather.
She carried him around the fenced run and sure enough,
the door stood open.

She flung him into the dim interior and stared at the
door. It had, as she now remembered from her first view
of the quarters, a round white china knob. Possibly Dirk
hadn't closed it quite tightly enough when he'd left, and
some inquisitive dog had nosed it open. She slammed it
with more irritation than she usually felt about anything,
because the first drops of rain were spattering down and
Nana was missing—and, come to think of it, Pushy—and
she had nineteen hounds that belonged to a friend and
were loose and would not answer to any call she could try.
"Drat!" said Julie, going off at her fastest clip to collect
dogs.

It was a long, arduous process until, after capturing
seven of them, she happened to see the big glass jar of
bacon fat where she'd left it beside the run, and instantly
hatched a plan. She toted it over to where the hounds were
gamboling—what a piece of luck, she thought, that they

hadn't decided to follow Nana into whatever distances the little beagle had plummeted—and set it down. Two came over, wagging their tails furiously, to thrust their noses into it. She clasped them firmly and covered the jar with the lid and got the couple back to join their jailed brothers. "Nine," she said, panting by now and very damp. The rain wasn't heavier, but the drops seemed to be getting larger.

She saw Pushy sitting with his customary patience beside the car. She ran over and put him into it, rolled down the window several inches to let him breathe, went back to discover the dripping-jar lidless and the top nowhere in sight, while five hounds tried to shove their muzzles into it all at once. She got two of them and rekenneled them, then two more. Some hound was evidently off in the bushes slurping at the missing lid. She collected the rest of them by ones and twos, while the level of fat gradually lowered in the big container. At last she thought she had them all safe inside. She got in out of the thickening rain and counted them three times. There were nineteen.

Growling under her wheezy breath, she went out looking, calling through the rolls of thunder. A lean young hound came dubiously toward her, whimpering with lonesomeness. He was led by the scruff to his home and given a pat of satisfaction and shut in; there was no lock on this door, only the knob. Julie made sure that it was tightly closed and absolutely couldn't be opened by anything but a human, and tramped stolidly back to the car, collecting the open jar of drippings on her way. She slid in beside Pushy and said *Whe-ew!* as he looked at her mournfully.

"That's that! Now for Nana, and home," she said, gasping. She realized how extremely uncomfortable she was, sopping and short of wind. "What a day this turned out to be," she said, starting her car and driving off slowly, windshield wipers flashing, toward the house.

In front of its forbidding door she stopped and turned off the engine. "I hate to do this to you, Pushy," she said, fondling his enormous head, "but I can't find her alone, I'd make book on that! Search, boy! Find Nana! Go find beagle!"

Pushy, long experienced and expert in this duty, rolled out into the rain and went lolloping off around the house, barking in great deep bursts of roaring sound. Julie headed the other way, calling at the top of her lungs, and circled the house. The fields lay silent and unyielding of beagles, the woods beyond gave her no response. She went up and stood on the covered porch, indecisive. Certainly she couldn't leave without Nana; she might never see the dear little monster again!

Lightning flashed, less than a mile away. The rain grew thicker, the atmosphere darker. And both dogs were missing now. Julie picked up the drippings jug and set it inside the unlocked door in the hall. Then she resolutely threw back her wet blond hair and set off into the fields, calling and calling. This time she covered more land, but finally the lightning was too close and the storm too downright miserable to keep at it, and she returned to her car.

She turned the key, thinking that the sound of the engine might bring the dogs on the run. It did not start. She fiddled and turned and pressed the gas pedal. "Oh, brother!" she said, wishing she were eight years younger so that she could cry.

The automobile was dead.

Chapter 9

Taking her purse from the seat, she emerged once more and walked slowly up onto the porch. She could not possibly be any wetter. She shook herself experimentally, like a dog coming out of a river, and a little spray flew off. She pressed her hair flat and ran her hands down it, succeeding in chilling her spine with the brook that gushed out from the long yellow mop. There being no other person idiotic enough to be out in this downpour, she took off her shirt and wrung a pint of water from it, then her jeans; and put them back on, damp but not oozing.

The wind subtly changed its direction, and rain began gusting in across the porch. Julie decided that the house, however grim, was the better place to be until the storm passed. If the storm was going to pass, she added, glancing at the sooty sky. She went inside and closed the door.

It was like shutting her two dogs out. She opened it a crack. The wind snatched it from her fingers and slammed it inward against the wall. She fought it closed again. Push and Nana would be under the trees somewhere for sure, waiting till the rain slacked.

She walked through the house, knowing that Dirk would not consider it prying. She'd only been in here two or three times, briefly, in all these weeks, and was curious to see how much work had been accomplished. Dirk had had a crew of carpenters and cleanup men here for a few days, but they had barely made a dent in the oddly ancient, deserted feel of the place. It was clean, and fortunately weatherproof, and one or two doors were off their hinges for rehanging; the old rugs were all gone, and a couple of floors sanded, and that was all.

She made sure that the kitchen door was shut firmly,

remembering Dirk's evident carelessness with the kennel knob. Then she checked on all the windows, upstairs and down. The last room that she entered was one she had not seen before: it was situated across from that in which she and Monty had first been welcomed by the Markhams, just off the main hall and on the right of the entrance. This was the nicest room in the house. She flicked the wall switch experimentally, and two lamps went on, shedding a rosy, warm, and *dry* glow on the surroundings.

There was no rug, but a vast leather easy chair, several antique tables, a fine modern sofa, and an enormous chest invited her to stay a while till she'd waited out the storm. Beyond the windows, which were nearly as tall as doors and opened onto the porch, the day was black as twilight and random bolts of lightning still shattered the heavens. Julie sat down in the leather chair, which wouldn't be marred by her dampness, and curled up her bare feet (having shucked her soaked shoes in the hall) beneath her.

Dirk had not put in a telephone yet. He'd said to her, laughing, "I'm never indoors to answer it!" That prohibited getting in touch with Fieldstone. Julie was not worried, however. The ghost legend bothered her less than a fly would have, the house was nowhere near so creepy inside as out, and except for the dogs she was content to wait until she was missed. That would be about nine o'clock, when Leon and Stash went down to check the horses. Then they'd know she hadn't merely dawdled at the Croydon chores, and worry, and come over to hunt for her.

If only Nana and Pushy were back by then! She got up and went to the windows, but there was no sign of them. The car sat there looking useless. What could be the matter with it? she wondered. "Flooded," she murmured, not knowing exactly what that meant; but anything might be flooded in that rain. She padded back to the chair and looked around again. On the chest stood a fine old oil lamp, filled and plainly in working order. Her father would love that. . . . Next time he came down from Ohio to visit, she'd bring him over and introduce him to Dirk, show him all the lovely antiques. . . . He owned an antique store, after all. . . .

Julie's head drooped back and she fell asleep.

When she woke with a start, she thought at first she'd only dozed for a few minutes, for the rain still beat against the house. But a look at her watch told her it was past nine. "Glory! I must have been *beat!*" she said aloud. She got out of the chair, happy to find that she had dried off in the hours that had gone by, and limped stiffly to the big windows. She opened one and felt the mist of the rain on her face as she leaned out and called, "Nana! Pushy! Are you there?" No joyous bark answered her. After a moment she closed the window. She wandered around the room, admiring the splendid old wooden floor. What a shame, though—there were dark old stains here by the fireplace. Maybe they'd come out with sanding.

Stains. Fireplace. It clicked. "Why, this is the study!" she exclaimed. "Where the murders happened!" Then, cocking her head, "Who am I talking to?" And she didn't want to think about that. Or about what had happened here so many years ago. Not so many at that. She wasn't too sure of the date, but she knew that it had been after she herself was born.

"Ain't no ghosts," she muttered. She went to the door and peered out into the murky hallway. She'd stay here, it was the cheerfulest room in the house despite its sad history, and suddenly the rest of the place seemed ominous, aware of her.

She began to close the door, but it had been warped by the seasons of neglect and would not shut properly. "You'd think they'd have taken this one off the hinges too," she said. "Probably didn't get this far yet." She left it half open and went to the window to call again.

Where could they be? Surely the storm that was now dying couldn't be the same one during which she'd fallen asleep. There must have been a lull, and this was another. What had happened to the scatterbrained beagle and the trustworthy St. Bernard? Had they given her up and started walking to Fieldstone? No, they wouldn't have done that with her car out there. Or maybe they would. A dog puts facts together in a different way from that of a human.

The wind shifted and blew straight in upon her, nearly ripping the hair off her head; the half-open door slammed shut with a reverberating crash that seemed to shiver the house. She shoved the window down and went to the door. It was tight shut. She tugged on the knob and nothing happened, not even a groan from the heavy wood. She set her bare feet firmly apart and threw everything she had into a pull—which had considerable force, thanks to her work with the horses—but it would not budge. She tried again and again, till she realized that she was growing frantic. Then she stopped and went over to stand by a lamp and consider. She could step out the window onto the porch and come in the front door again, but that would mean, with the wind at such a furious height, that she would be drenched again. She didn't fancy that.

There was a flash of lightning and an earthshaking crash on its heels, and the electricity went off. The room was pitch, a big threatening cauldron of tar in which she stood almost afraid to breathe. Then she said loudly, "Oh, good grief!" and began to grope toward the chest and the oil lamp.

She thought she remembered seeing a matchbook beside it. Maybe that was just hopefulness, but—

Now what?

There was a sound in the hall.

"Stash!" she cried happily. "Leon! I knew you'd come!"

No shout answered her. The noise approached from the rear of the house, down the long hallway toward the study door. She was adjusting to the darkness now; she could make out the furniture dimly and the windows were pale oblongs. She watched the door, hypnotized. The noise came on.

It was the sound of someone walking slowly toward her in bedroom slippers. Sssh-flap, sssh-flop, on it came. Julie felt suddenly and completely terrified, and all her scorn of ghosts and such myths evaporated. She began to imagine what it looked like. A squeak of horror escaped her, and she clapped a hand over her mouth.

It halted in front of her door.

"L-l-leon?"

After what felt like a long time, the sound resumed, and grew fainter as whatever-it-was went back down the hall to the kitchen. Julie groped over to the chest and touched cautiously until her fingers closed on the matchbook. She lit a match, took the chimney off, and lit the oil lamp, throwing the room into a mass of weaving shadows and yellow glowings. Under the circumstances, it was better than the gloom of night.

She looked at the door. Imagination? No! By no means whatever could sane, practical Julie Jefferson conjure up a sound that wasn't there. And she knew it.

"What was it?" she whispered, and jerked her head around abruptly as though something might answer her out of the corner or from the fireplace.

Making sure that the lamp was out of the way of any wind that might come in, she opened the window again. She was stranded here, yes, but only so long as she feared a drenching more than the thing that made noises in the hall. She had no fear of the study, in spite of its reputation. But *noises* . . .

Old floor boards creak at night, but not in a rhythmical pattern that simulates a man walking slowly in slippers.

The wet out there was real, and the eeriness of the night too; though with the thunderbolt that had put out the light, the electrical storm had subsided, leaving the world to rain and wind alone.

Her purse and shoes were out in the hall.

She could step out the window, go to the front door, go into the hall—

"On the whole," she told herself aloud, "I'd rather stay here and think good thoughts." Which was difficult enough, she added silently, to give anybody pause.

She walked a few steps into the room, leaving the window open to air the place out (or was it for a quick escape, in case? She hardly knew), and there was a whoosh and thud behind her, and she shrieked and whirled round to see the largest, wettest St. Bernard in Kentucky.

"Oh, Pushy!"

She hugged him despite his condition, and he forgot

manners so far as to lick her face with his enormous tongue. He looked dead beat and wretched, but pleased to see his mistress. "Where have you been, you scoundrel? And where's Nana?" She pulled him over by the window, where the floor was already damp, and pressed as much rain out of his coat as she could. Then she ruffled his fur to help it dry quicker, and went back, enormously heartened now that she wasn't alone, to try the door again.

Behind her the sound came: sssh-flip, sssh-flop. Instantly she knew what it was, and burst into a peal of laughter that was just on the edge of hysteria.

A St. Bernard shuffling across a bare wooden floor sounds precisely like an old man in bedroom slippers.

Pushy was the answer to the question; he had come down the hall, scented her, and gone out again to enter by the window. That left only one more question—

"How'd you get into the house in the first place?" she demanded.

Pushy gazed up at her drearily and gave no reply.

"Come sit over here, and pretend there's a fire," she said, sitting down crosslegged on the hearth. He did so. They sat together for five or ten minutes, communing without words.

There was a knock. A single, muffled knock.

The dog raised his head.

"Well, I didn't imagine it, then," said Julie with a slight tremor in her voice. "Is it someone at the door, do you think?"

A double knock, somewhat nearer, answered her. "More toward the kitchen," she said, distinctly wavery now. "The slippers were you—who's the knocking?"

A vision of Nana banging something came and went; this was the sound of a hard object rapped briskly against a wall or floor.

"Oh, do you suppose we'll *have* to go sit in the car till they come? It's locked, and the keys are in my purse, and the purse is out in the hall, and it's so damp outside and you're just getting dry! We won't do it. We'll stick this out together." She put her arm around the giant dog. "What's a knock, anyway? Can't hurt us."

Crash!

"Oh, dear," said Julie.

The wind shifted and the rain sheeted in. She flew to close the window. The room was quieter when the rain's pounding was muted, and the series of quick thuds were closer, clearer, louder.

She knew that no car had driven up, no door opened and slammed, but she boldly called out, "Stash? Leon? I'm in here, and the door won't open." And the perfect chaos of bangs and bumps that followed seemed to answer her, *I know you're in there.*

Now it stopped, and then began again, like weird smashing footsteps up and down the hall. Clutching Pushy, she said, "The slippers were natural, the crashes just *have* to be too! But natural who, or what?"

It was not an animal sound. She reminded herself that she'd have said that about the first ghost. But this wasn't!

Crash! from the vicinity of the kitchen.

Pushy broke away from her and, beside himself, pounced to the door, snuffled wildly, prowled back and forth, tried the window and found it shut, returned to the door. Julie gripped his heavy collar and said, "You silly dog, stop fussing! What if it hears you—"

Then she knew that she was afraid, and that she might not believe in ghosts but she did believe firmly in the possible danger of unidentified sounds.

And the noise racketed out, just outside the study door, and she retreated, hauling Pushy with her and shaking with dread.

"If only the rain would stop." Yet if it did, how was she to retrieve her car keys? The thing was out there, all over the hallway, knocking and thumping and clunking and smashing until she thought she'd soon scream. "I won't," she said to the St. Bernard. "I'm a grown and responsible person and I won't scream." He looked at her, wagging his tail. "And I won't desert you, and I won't have you out in the rain, and oh, Pushy, why won't it stop?"

She glanced at the lamp; it held enough oil for the rest of the night. The racket suddenly ceased. She held her

breath. Silence, so deep that she could hear the oil sizzling
in the wick. Was the rain slackening?

She sat on the edge of the easy chair, far from easy
herself. The stillness lengthened into a quarter of an hour.
Pushy lay down and composed his paws properly and went
to sleep.

The window smashed with a bursting tinkle and crack
that jolted her right off the chair. The glass fell on the
wooden floor and a large rock rolled over and stopped
short of her feet. Pushy was up and running; Julie caught
him just before he went through the broken window. She
thought a figure moved swiftly down the driveway from
the house, but in that murk she couldn't be sure. The
wind sighed in, calmer now than before. The noise in the
hall began all over.

"I will not go out of my head," said Julie loudly. "I
don't care what you do. I may be as flapped as I've ever
been, but I'm staying here and that's *that!*"

She soothed Pushy and commanded him to lie down by
the imaginary fire, which at last he did. She picked up the
rock and examined it; it was in no way extraordinary. She
threw it out of the window.

"Ghosts don't throw rocks. Ghosts don't bang solidly
up and down a hall, either, because they aren't there to
begin with. There's a perfectly normal explanation for all
of this. But it beats me," she sighed, "what it can be."

Half an hour dragged by, with the noise occurring and
stopping erratically. Pushy was now ignoring it.

"It couldn't be a loose shutter, could it? Not unless it's
so loose that it's running up and down the hall. . . ."

She found that she was no longer truly afraid. It had
gone on too long, was too pointless; it didn't threaten her
any longer. Once, now, when it thumped out suddenly
after a long hush, she actually laughed. And just after
that, she heard a car drive up and saw the headlights.

"Now it'll stop," she told Pushy, "and we'll never know.
Not that I *want* to know, specially." She leaned out the
window. "Hi!" she called loudly. Then, as figures came
toward the porch, she unlatched the frame and pushed it

up so that no one would be cut on the shattered glass. "Who is it?"

"Everybody in creation," said Leon's calm voice, "except maybe Whirlaway and Native Dancer." His fine old face showed in the oil lamp's beam as he bent and oozed into the study. "Monty's here, he came home tonight, and Stash—what's going on, Julie girl? How come this window's busted, and you're here all alone?"

She told him in bursts of words as she hugged him, then Stash, then Monty. "And I knew you'd come, but that racket in the hall just set my teeth on edge!"

"We'll soon see what it is," he assured her. "Good thing Monty got worried, though, 'cause Stash and I were goin' to go to bed, thinking you were just visitin' late and would come home in your own time."

"I don't hear anything in the hall," said Monty practically.

"Well, not now, silly," the girl said. "It stopped when it heard you coming."

There was a single reverberating thud.

"See?" said Julie, gesturing placidly. "It wants you to know it's real."

The three men tore at the thick door, and with many hands on the knob somehow hauled it open, the wood screeching. Three flashlights clicked on and illuminated the hallway.

Julie waited behind them, holding her breath.

Monty began to choke with helpless laughter..

"Oh, you oaf! What *is* it?"

"The Phantom of Croydon Farm, or, Ghastly Gertrude the Ghostly Ghoul," said Monty, blocking her view on purpose. "Make a wild guess."

It could be only one small creature, when he made a joke of it that way. She said, incredulous, "Nana?"

"Nana," nodded Leon, grinning. They let her out to see.

In the beams of the flashlights, there stood a very sheepish and uncomfortable beagle, her head firmly wedged into the glass jug of bacon drippings (now all but empty). "There's your greedy little spook," said Monty, and assisted the dog to free herself with gentle, practiced fingers.

"She'll need some tidying up—she's grease from ears to nose tip. It's a miracle, considering how long she spent clunking it against the walls and floor, that she didn't break the jar and hurt herself."

Julie retrieved her shoes and purse, shaking her head severely at her beagle. The question of how Nana and Pushy had gotten themselves into the house was half-solved by the open kitchen door, which she shut once more. But how had it come open—how had the kennel door come open, too—and had Julie really seen a dim figure running down the driveway?

It made no sense; but considering what the men's response would probably be—after her two ghosts had turned into dogs—to a phantom rock-thrower, Julie decided not to even mention it.

There'd be enough jokes to grin weakly under, as it was!

Chapter 10

The engine started at the first tentative try. She gazed at them from her window. "It was dead," she said defensively.

"Heavens above, girl, we believe you," said Monty. "Go ahead, we'll follow you back home."

She'd left a note for Dirk, explaining that the window had been broken in the storm; which was true, of course, and only left out the mysterious rock. All the way back to Fieldstone she worried at the problems, and couldn't solve one of them. She *had* tested the kitchen door. Dirk would *not* have been careless enough to leave the kennel door ajar. She *knew* she'd seen someone running from the house after the rock had come in. Lex wasn't due till tomorrow, and Dirk was away.

Who? Who? Who?

Maybe she or one of the men should have stayed at Croydon overnight. Maybe some vandal . . .

Nothing made any sense.

Julie shook her head, glanced at the sleeping dogs beside her, and tried to put it all out of her mind.

Monty, it turned out, was on vacation, having brought home a long string of winners at the track and richly earned some time off. Dan Gibson had by now received his trainer's license and was taking over until Mr. T decided that Monty had rested enough. So he mooched around the farm, helping with this and that, and seeing more of Julie in a few days than he had for half a year.

Julie, mindful of what Stash had said, was more attentive than usual to Monty, and he began to think that he'd been wrong to suspect her of a deep interest in Dirk Markham. The few days stretched into a week, then two; Julie was becoming more and more caught up in the concept of jumping horses, but now she went to Croydon, put Cache through his paces, and returned to tell Monty all about it. For his part, the young trainer managed to whip up a kind of interest in what she was doing, and studied enough to make intelligent responses to her babblings, and for the first time in ages felt that he and the girl were growing close once more.

"But you would never want to leave racing for the shows, would you?" he asked anxiously.

She thought a moment. "No. No, I wouldn't. With Bonnie, and then with Deerstalker, and even some of Mr. T's other racehorses, no, I wouldn't ever leave racing. It's first with me. But I'm—well, impressed, excited, thrilled, inquisitive about the act of jumping fences on horseback. It sounds weird when I say it straight out that way, but . . . you know?"

"I know. I've listened to you enough to know," said Monty. "It's probably good for you to diversify your horse interests. Some of us become so wrapped up in the track that we don't see or do anything else, ever. That's too confining—it makes for a narrow person."

"What else do you live and breathe except racing?"

"Don't look so anxious about me," said Monty, smiling. "I read a lot of good books, and I think a lot about you."

Julie got out of her chair and came over to where he sat in her kitchen drinking coffee, and kissed him. It was the first time she'd ever done it except in the high excitement of getting a new horse or running a fine race, and he was a little taken aback, but immensely pleased. He stood up and kissed her back. Then she disengaged herself comfortably and sat down again.

"I'll have to think about all this," she said quietly.

"All what?" he teased.

"Racing and showing, silly," she teased in return. "Just talking about it makes me remember what a thrill you can get from a race, especially if you're in the saddle. I might take a run down to Florida one of these days."

"What? Why?"

"Remember, I hold a jockey's license there," she said.

"And I do *love* racing. Running with the wind, with the fastest living thing on earth under you—at least, the fastest critter you can throw a saddle on—feeling all that tremendous power flashing down the track, the ground-devouring strides, the terrible chance you're taking of going down under the hoofs that are slamming along behind you—"

"I notice that you're in the lead," said Monty.

"Always. Or coming up on the outside after a slow start to take the lead, that's great too. If only Bonnie can make her comeback!"

"I have a feeling that she will. That leg has healed, from all that Doc and Leon and Stash and I can tell, as good as it ever was. Very few mares come back after foaling," he said judiciously, "but Bonnie, well, she just might. Not many horses like her in a generation."

"Not many in history," said Julie, firm of jaw. "I'm not going to breed her back to Tweedy, Monty. I'm going to wait till the foals are weaned, and then start her on a program of—hey! it's time to go school Cache!" She was up and out in a rush, leaving Monty to sit over his cooling coffee and think very hard indeed.

Julie drove up to the parking place at Croydon and got out just in time to watch Alexis, who had come home the day before, jump down through a line of fences in such perfect form that Julie was left breathless with wonder that a girl and horse could perform so flawlessly. She ran to congratulate Dirk's sister.

"That was fantastic! Welcome home," she added, as Lex trotted up to where her brother had been standing and watching her work.

"Hi, Julie. Was I all right?" she asked Dirk almost anxiously.

"I never thought I'd see the day when Mother Moose would come down a line like that!" he told her. "That filly," he said to Julie, "was the most uncoordinated beast I'd ever seen. As you might guess from her nickname."

"We have one at Fieldstone I call Hippopotamare."

"Give her to Lex for training. I thought more than once that this brute would get Lex killed, and she fell with her more times than the law allows, but now look at her!

Can't manage to put a foot wrong. Lex, I think she's ready to hit a show or two, to see whether she'll lose her cool. If she doesn't, and goes as she did that last trip, then you'll be the one to beat for certain."

Lex's face brightened with pleasure. Julie added some verbal applause of her own, reaching out to pat the filly; but Lex wheeled her away almost rudely, mumbling something about not standing around with hot horses, and that she was going to give her a bath. "I'll hold her while you wash," Julie offered.

"No thanks," said Alexis, and walked the filly off toward the barn.

"I'd love to watch your sister do a whole workout some day," said Julie wistfully. "She's such a natural-born rider. I could pick up tips."

"If she seems cool or even hostile, don't take it personally, dear girl. Something's bugging her." He dismissed the topic with a shrug. "Well, what have you in mind for today, Julie?"

"When you say it in that tone of voice, you always have your own mind made up. You know what fascinates me: the open jumping phase of schooling."

"That is, you find the bigger fences and more difficult courses a tougher challenge, and the notion of showing and jumping high, wide, and colorful courses in the jumper division is more appealing to you than just riding around the show hunter courses where all the jumps for a horse's first year are three-feet-six." He patted her on the head affectionately. "You must walk, you know, before you can run. You must jump small before you leap big."

Because she respected him, she listened; nonetheless, there remained a yearning in her to find out whether Cache might not have an undetected and absolutely phenomenal jumping ability that would justify her schooling him over the taller fences when the proper time came.

Cache was making good progress, and Julie was an apt pupil, as Dirk frequently told her. The gray's work on the flat had progressed remarkably, mainly due to her perseverence and dedication to not missing a day. He was now quite well balanced, and though he sometimes made a mistake with his right lead, by and large he got it correctly when asked for it. Julie was also jumping some small fences with him from the trot; Dirk had long since told her that she mustn't allow him to canter to his fences till he was completely relaxed and confident in jumping from the trot.

"You can always increase his speed," Dirk had dinned into her, "but it takes the devil's own time to make him slow down, once he has the idea that he must have speed in order to jump." They had been working mainly with small single fences, some three feet to three-feet-three in height, which were "square." That meant that the jump was composed of two elements set parallel to each other. This was so he'd learn to jump in a wider arc than would normally be required to negotiate a single element, and would be better prepared to handle any sort of obstacle. Once he'd been schooled over square fences for a while, he would come to expect the second element on every fence, whether it was there or not, and would have learned to jump "round" and in good form instead of "flat" and hurried.

Julie had also been jumping the first step in the simple-gymnastic department, which consisted of a placement fence—either a cross rail or small straight rail—and then a measured distance to a square fence. The idea of that was that the placement fence, set from twelve to eighteen feet before the second, would put the horse in perfect position for the second fence no matter how he happened to arrive at it—on stride, off stride, or something in between. Cache was handy at these gymnastics and Julie was learning in her very bones to sit still and let the horse do the jumping, so that by this time she could ride through these arrangements with ease and confidence. Gymnastics are excellent confidence-builders for both horse and rider; Julie and Cache were progressing together in their self-assurance.

Now Dirk said to her, "Before we get Cache and Soul-searching, I want to make some changes in the schooling fences. I do intend to start something new today. You wait while I go to the barn and get my tape measure."

"I have a ruler in the car."

He laughed. "A hundred-foot tape in a metal case is what we need, silly." He hared off and returned with one. "Come help set up, honey-hair," he said lightly.

She had come well past the stage of blushing at these endearing and complimentary names, and took them in stride. "What do we do?"

"Dismantle some fences and drag poles, wings, brush boxes, and so forth from here to there, or there to here if that helps. I wish Lex hadn't vanished like that," he said, beginning to work at the construction of his fences. "I told her I wanted to build a couple of little gymnastics, and that it might take three of us, but she up and disappeared again."

"Her horse needed a bath."

"Not all that badly. Sometimes I worry about her, Julie. She's alone so much of the time, so much more withdrawn and quiet since we came to Croydon."

I wonder, thought Julie suddenly, if Lex has had experiences here like mine? If maybe someone chucked a rock at her too? I wonder . . . I wonder if she thinks that it might have been *me?*

"Lex used to have such a sunny disposition," Dirk was saying between grunts as they lifted an obstacle. "That's part of the reason I decided to find a larger farm. More room for her to stretch in, more things for that busy mind to tangle with. Oh, maybe she's only tired out from the Connecticut-New York circuit. She did so well that I suppose it was worth it for her, but she tends to drive herself to extremes. Let's put this there."

"Let's," agreed Julie, puffing.

When he had all the necessary components assembled, Dirk handed Julie the end of the tape, and carefully measured eighteen feet. "Stay right there," he said, and marked a large cross in the dirt. He then came back to her side and with her help had shortly constructed a simple, single-element, vertical fence about three feet high. Then they went to the X in the dirt, and there he built a small oxer, which consisted of parallel rails at three-feet-three, with a pony-sized brush box between them.

Again he had Julie hold the tape, and this time measured thirty-two feet, at which point he constructed another small and attractive fence, a white pony-sized gate with a rail behind it, also about three-feet-three.

The next measurement was forty-six feet, at which distance Dirk briskly assembled a second oxer, this one with a pony-sized stone wall set between the rails. He still had plenty of rails piled nearby, and Julie was ready to ask what they were going to do with them or should she move them out of the way, when Dirk elected her anchor man once more and measured off thirty-six feet. At this final spot he constructed the last fence of his gymnastic: four or five rails laid closely atop one another for the first element, then a single rail parallel with the top of the first one for the other half. In front of this he set an eight-inch brush box for a ground line, as he explained to Julie. The slant of the white gate, the brush box, and the stone wall provided a ground line of sorts that would help their horses to judge the fences; but the plain rails that he'd just set up would prove more difficult, and since his aim was to bolster the horses' confidence and not to confuse them, he was thus helping them by adding a very definite ground line.

They strung out the tape between them and, Dirk in the lead, remeasured each of the distances from fence to fence. Satisfied, he said, "Now that you see how it's measured off with the tape, come walk it with me and see how close you can come to the actual footage."

He caught her hand and led her back to the first simple fence. "Let me show you how you can get a fair notion of the distance between any number of fences without tugging out your tape all the time. Assuming that the average horse—and I know Bonnie does better, so don't tell me!—the *average* horse covers twelve feet with each cantering stride, provided that he isn't cantering in a teacup . . ."

"Doing what?"

"Cantering very slowly with little mincing steps. And knowing that he needs room for take-off and landing on either side, it isn't too hard to learn to 'walk off' or pace any distance between fences. It's helpful, too, to know that the average distance for one stride in an in-and-out is twenty-four feet, which accounts for twelve feet for the stride itself plus about six feet each for take-off and landing.

"Of course, if your fences are only two-feet-six, you can't expect a horse to go into the air six feet in advance and to land six feet beyond; so you have to adjust your calculations accordingly. If you practice walking off three-foot distances for a while, you'll be able to pace and convert into horse strides easily. So! Let's try your skill and luck with this gymnastic."

Gamely Julie began pacing off the distance between obstacles. She knew that it was eighteen feet from the first to the second: that was one stride, and had been made eighteen feet because Dirk meant to trot to the first part, and if he'd made this the standard twenty-four, it would have been much too far for the horses to do in one stride—furthermore, since none of the fences were very high, three-feet-three for most of them, he'd shortened the distances to keep it easy for their mounts. Julie tried, and guessed it aloud at nineteen feet, and went back and paced it again and a third time, until she felt that "eighteen feet even!" was her honest estimate and not simply an echo of what she knew it to be.

"Good. Go ahead." Dirk was pacing beside her, watching with his customary admiring stare.

"Stop looking at me or you'll rattle me," she said.

"That's good news," he said; "you notice me even when you're concentrating on something else."

"Oh, do shut up," said Julie, and detected a rather fond note in her own voice and was a bit jolted by it. She paced from the oxer to the white gate with the rail. "Thirty-two feet, or, let's see, two strides?"

"On the nose."

She got the forty-six feet to the oxer with the stone wall all right, but goofed on the last distance from over-confidence and had to do it over. "Thirty-six, therefore, two strides. But why thirty-six here and thirty-two back there?"

"I made the last distance a little longer because the

horse should meet it cantering, and because the last obstacle is about three-feet-four."

"I see. Can we get the horses now?"

"Instantly."

They went up to the barn, Julie feeling the glow of excitement as well as the crawly skin-ripple of anxiety at the thought of Cache attacking his first real gymnastic. Dirk talked, as they got out their tack and worked with the horses, of how helpful gymnastics were in schooling mounts and teaching them to adjust to different distances and to different types of fences. "Once a horse gains confidence and can handle himself through varying gymnastics, with anything from no strides to five or six between fences, without changing his pace or altering his jumping form, then he can do just about anything you could want from him. I've probably told you this before, and will again—if I bore you, Julie, please tell me—but you must never, absolutely *never* ride through any gymnastic or obviously premeasured line of fences without first familiarizing yourself with the existing distances."

"You never bore me, and yes, you've said it before, but it'll stick in my skull better now that we're actually going to ride through that course, and since we've paced it so thoroughly."

"Good. It might be okay on some occasions with an old and experienced horse, but with a greenie, the slightest change or a tricky distance can turn a schooling device into a surefire trap. Keep that firmly in your mind. And even when you know what the distances are, you have to have a fair notion of your horse's ability too, because if he isn't up to handling the combination of spans, then again you could trap him."

"I wouldn't think of approaching any gymnastic without your approval for a long time to come," Julie told him, swinging into her saddle, "if *ever*!"

That appeared to satisfy him. He obviously believed wholeheartedly in his methods of schooling, and from the number of superior show horses that he'd produced, on his own and with his sister, he knew whereof he spoke.

They worked Cache and Soul-searching on the flat for

a while, and all went well until with a neigh and a twitch,
the dark bay with the four white stockings and the white
nose went into what could only be called a fit of temper,
and did his best to unseat Dirk with every buck, twist, and
sunfish maneuver that he could command. Julie, appalled,
kept Cache well back from the tornado until it had spun
itself out and Soul-searching stood quiet, head hanging
and a guilty I'm-sorry-I-won't-do-it-again look in his eye.
Dirk dismounted and said a few words to him, and the
bay grumbled plaintively through his nose. Then they
walked over to Julie.

"He thinks he's a real outlaw," said Dirk, somewhat
winded but smiling.

"That was spectacular, and I'm sorry he isn't cured of
it," Julie said, "but it was almost worth it to see you
handle him! You were great!"

"Glue on the saddle is the secret. Look, I sure don't
want to send him through the gymnastic after that. I never
use the bat on him, but he knows when I'm angry and
he'll be wavering in his mood, and the degree of his attention, for quite a spell now. You go ahead with Cache.
Work him over some of those placement fences with only
one jump after them, as you have been doing, and then
I'll watch you through the gymnastic."

Julie did as she was told until Cache was thoroughly
warmed up. Then her friend signaled her to him. "Okay,
go on down there and let him slip through that gymnastic
one time. I want to see how he'll handle it on his own, so
don't you help him. Just go along for the ride. You'll want
a lively trot to the first piece, but let him do the rest. It
should ride out an easy one stride, two strides, three
strides, two. After he lands over the last fence, don't let
him turn right or left, but just sit down easy and pull up
in a straight line. We don't want him to get the habit of
drifting off any-old-where after he's been in a line of
fences. Let's go, Julie."

She took the gray a little distance from the fence line
and put him into a lively trot. She circled once, to make
sure he was listening, and that she'd established a steady
cadence; then she straightened him and headed for the

center of the first fence, the simple single-element three-foot fence that began the run.

Cache met it beautifully, and landed perfectly in line to negotiate the second. As Dirk had predicted, there was precisely the right amount of level dirt for one easy stride and then he was in the air again, sailing over the brush-box oxer. Julie had a fleeting picture of a great winged bird, and her toes tingled, but she snapped herself back to the business at hand as he landed, steadied himself for the obvious two strides that lay between him and the third fence, and went on.

Taking the white gate easily and without flaw, Cache gave her the feeling that he was beginning to enjoy this new game, which offered him the chance to bound into the air every stride or so.

"Mustn't get overanxious," Julie cautioned herself, "just sit still and wait for the fence to happen." How often had Dirk used that phrase?

Land and wait for three. Isn't Cache wonderful? Going straight and true and effortlessly as a well-aimed arrow. As if he'd been doing it all his life. Wouldn't dream of stopping. Plenty of sugar for him at the end of this day.

She felt him thrust off the ground over the stone-walled oxer and land like a puff of cloud on the further side. Two strides and—

Too late, she saw with a burst of horror that there was no way to meet the last fence.

It had all gone so smoothly until then that even Cache was taking things as they came, and certainly not watching for a trappy distance. He took one stride and, knowing somehow that there wasn't space for another, tried to leave the ground from the position in which he found himself. But there was room neither for two strides nor for one, but something in between. To accomplish what he was trying desperately to do, Cache would have needed greater speed, more impulsion, or a higher fence behind and before him.

He left the ground as best he could, not from neatly gathered hindquarters as he always had, but with his quarters sprawled behind him, giving little if any thrust to his great body. He made a valiant attempt to save himself, stabbing blindly at the jump, to no avail. He met his arc just as he met the five-rail fence, and in a dreadful tangle of rails, standards, wings and tack, poor Cache somersaulted into the final element of the gymnastic.

Luckily for Julie, the horse's wild attempts to save himself and the impact of his collision had sent her flying headforemost out of the saddle, and though she hit the ground hard and rolled a yard or two, she came up only shaken, a little bruised, and with one cheekbone skinned raw.

She scrambled over to her horse, who was standing now and looking at her with a very blank expression. He seemed all right—he was, miraculously, all right, only shaken—and Julie let out a wheeze of relief.

Dirk ran up. "I saw it all," he said, looking distracted and pale. "I saw it from the side, and knew from the way he was going that it would work out perfectly. But it didn't. Are you okay?"

"Sure. So's he."

Dirk instantly began to pace off the distance between the wreckage of the last obstacle and the fourth, intact fence. "Thirty feet?" he shouted, and paced it back again. "Thirty feet! Julie, it can't be. We measured it twice and paced it twice! I don't understand," he said, staring around as though there had to be an explanation of the accident sitting there for him to see. "It couldn't have happened."

"My paces were probably erratic," said Julie uncertainly.

"Well, I admit I didn't count paces, but yours were uniform within inches . . . and I sure did measure carefully. I don't get it." He walked on to the correct site for the five-rail and stared at the dirt thoughtfully. "No sign here of anything being moved," he mumbled. "Look, dear, you're in no state to ride this again, but Cache can't be left with a disaster like this in his mind, understand? We've got to wipe it out for him right away." He began to reconstruct the fifth fence at its proper distance. "Can't have him brooding and worrying, can we?"

"If you think he's up to doing it again," she said, dubious.

"Yes, he is. You go over and sit down and watch us." He mounted, still shaking his head, and trotted off with a scowl.

Julie sat down where she could view the course. She agreed with Dirk: it could not have happened, but it had happened.

As Dirk wheeled Cache toward the gymnastic, Julie heard a car drive up and stop beside her own. It was Monty in his old red Chevy. He came over at a run and knelt beside her. "Hi! Was going home from Meriden and thought I'd see how Cache was doing."

"Ssh," Julie shushed him.

"Hey, what's Dirk doing on him?"

"Please ssh," she repeated. "Tell you later."

"Right," said Monty, with the definite feeling that it wasn't.

They watched as Dirk sent the gray into a steady, brisk trot. Obviously he anticipated trouble, for no horse in its right mind would return blithely to the scene of such a crash. But Cache proved nobly that he was the exception to that rule, and except that Dirk had to drive him a little strongly from the wall to the last rail fence on the first and second time he went through, by the third run he was plainly growing confident; and on the fourth and final attempt, Cache all but did it on his own.

"Oh, bravo, Cache!" cried the girl, clapping.

"What happened to the piece of skin from your left cheek?" asked Monty, looking at her.

"I suppose it's lying out there somewhere," said Julie.

"What?"

"I fell, that's all."

"How?"

Alexis came from nowhere and said to them, "I came for Soul-searching, to take him up to the stable, if Dirk's going to be riding Cache instead."

"Soul-searching did a buck and wing," said Julie. "He won't be working any more today, thanks."

Dirk rode over to them. "Did you two see the spectacular tumble our Julie took?"

Lex shook her head, and Monty said, "No!" with a kind of bristle at the phrase *our Julie.*

So Dirk started in and told them all about it, including the unaccountably wrong measurements. Monty shifted and cleared his throat until Julie thought he would erupt, but said nothing. "Look," said Dirk to the blond girl, "I'll take care of Cache for you tonight. I'll set him up in bandages and that good blue liniment. He might be a little stiff come morning."

"I'd appreciate that," said Julie. "I think I'll be getting home and dip myself in some liniment too."

"See you tomorrow?"

"Absolutely. I've taken falls before."

"Good girl!" said Dirk, beaming.

With Monty in tow, she headed for their cars. "I have just one question," said that gentleman. "Who told you to ride over that bunch of fences, and why didn't he do it first, since he's so much more experienced than you?"

"His horse threw a jumping fit, I said! We hadn't any reason to think there'd be anything wrong. We still don't know how it happened."

"Jumping fit? I thought he was such a lamb? Maybe he had something sharp slipped under his saddle, like a burr?"

"Monty Everett, what's that supposed to suggest?"

"Oh, nothing. It all just sounds fishy to me."

"That's because you're a strictly racetrack man," said Julie. "And fences are never in a 'bunch'!"

"I'm a dismally stupid oaf," said Monty, and got into his car and drove away.

Chapter 11

For a week or more Dirk fussed over Julie's safety until she could have screamed at him, had she been the screaming type. It was "Julie, don't do that" and "Julie, be careful" and "Julie, you cannot jump anything higher than two-feet-six till I say so," and she thought it was all very childish and . . . well, verging on the ridiculous.

The two of them were in the tack room, cleaning tack. "You know, Julie, I've been watching you carefully for the past days—"

"I know," said Julie patiently.

"Oh, all right, I've been a mother hen! But I want to do all I can to better your techniques, methods, feel for the business, now don't I? I was wondering if you might not get a better sense of what's happening with the horse if you used a saddle with less padding. Those German saddles are fine for little old ladies who need to be locked into position, but as experienced as you are, there's simply too much leather between you and Cache for any real contact."

"I'm for anything that'll improve my riding," said Julie, brightening as she realized that it wasn't going to be a protective lecture. "I'll stop in at the saddlery shop in Meriden on my way here tomorrow and see what they have."

"Hold on! Have you any notion what a saddle—any saddle, good, bad, or mediocre—costs?"

"I've been buying saddles for a long time, Mr. Markham, sir."

"You can't just walk in and buy the first hunk of leather that strikes your fancy, though. Besides, you aren't even sure you'd like another kind."

"I have a jockey's license. I've ridden, oh, two or even three kinds of saddles!"

Dirk had the grace to chuckle. "You've undoubtedly ridden more varieties of saddle than I've ever seen. But I'm very serious about this. It's a big outlay if you aren't certain it's truly for you."

"Bonnie bought me all sorts of nice things when she was racing," countered Julie, "and I don't think she'd begrudge me a saddle if it would help me do better with Cache."

"That isn't the point," said Dirk patiently. "You ought to try a couple of different types before you decide on a specific saddle. I'm sure you don't have a show-type rig in your own collection—"

"Seein' as how I'm just a mis'able little racetrack brat," said Julie, feeling that this conversation tended to put her down rather too much.

"Well, for heaven's sake, look at mine! It's a French saddle, built on a steeplechase exercise tree. It weighs about nine pounds, and besides its particular construction it's so soft you could almost roll it up and stuff it in your pocket. Have you got anything like that?"

"No."

"After all, if you buy a saddle you've got to ride it, and if you decide afterwards that it's all wrong, you might get partial credit on it against another one . . . if they take in used saddles on trade at all in Meriden."

"What is a poor girl to do?" wailed Julie, putting down the soap and wringing her hands.

"Cut it out. You can try mine. Try it tomorrow, and for a few days, and see how you like it."

"Okay, if you really don't mind. I won't let anything happen to it, and I'll clean it when I'm through—"

"It is not the Hope diamond," said Dirk. "It cost a lot, but it's a saddle, and you treat it like any other saddle."

"Except with reverence."

Alexis appeared at the door of the tack room. "Hi," said Julie brightly. "We were just discussing the inadequacy of my saddle, and Dirk says I'd do better with one like yours."

"You've noticed that Lex's and mine are identical, then," said Dirk. "Good observation."

"You treat her as if she were eight years old," said Lex scornfully. "She's been riding longer than I have." Somehow she made it sound as though Julie were about ready to become a grandmother. But then the slight dark girl smiled, and the illusion of scornfulness was gone. Lex had a lovely smile. "Why don't you try mine, Julie? They're too expensive to buy without a trial, but an hour or two in mine ought to prove whether it's right for you."

"I just offered her mine, and she accepted," said Dirk, "but it's very good of you to suggest your own, dear."

"Either one will educate you, Julie," Lex said with a semblance of actual animation. "The less leather between horse and rider, the quicker you'll feel what he's going to do, the easier you can anticipate his next move. A rider can really get with a horse in the right saddle. I've wondered why you haven't gone to a lighter one before this."

"Until Dirk moved here, there really wasn't anyone to consult about riding show horses, and till I got Cache the idea never crossed my mind. The tiny exercise saddles we use at Fieldstone are nothing more than something to hang your irons on. When you're galloping horses," said Julie, warming to the subject, "you don't need to worry about contact, feel, those things, because you're not up there long enough, you know? And although we do give the young stock sort of an education before they go to the track, there's no such thing as 'collection' or 'extension,' or the kind of responsiveness that's required of a show horse, with them; I mean we don't teach the babies too much, the general belief around the track being that if you teach a horse too much, you'll take away some of his run."

"I don't know," said Alexis slowly, "but that seems like, well, like superstition! It doesn't make sense to me."

"Doesn't to me either!" agreed Julie. "But I have to contend with Monty, whose ideas of riding just echo his father's. There aren't many riding aspects to his life—he's a *trainer*—but he'd sure be appalled and start roaring if I broke or rode racers like show horses."

"The old must give place to the new eventually," put in Dirk solemnly, "and poor old Monty will some day have to recognize the fallacy in that teaching idea, I'm afraid."

"Poor old Monty is about six years younger than sprightly young Dirk," said Julie. "But some of his ideas are positively antediluvian."

"Antiquated old Dirk knows perfectly well that aged and gray Monty is younger, but the poor old buzzard was cracking a jest," said Dirk. "Not cutting up a rival behind his back, Julie."

"What's that mean?" demanded Lex.

"Getting back to saddles, I'll be glad to try yours, Dirk, tomorrow," said Julie hastily. She wanted to add that she wasn't out to snatch Lex's whole family away from her, but thought an instant and kept her mouth shut on that touchy subject. "I'd try yours, Lex, but you ride so much more than your brother, I'd feel I was depriving you."

Lex sat down on a bale and they began a long conversation on the saddle topic. It was far and away the longest they'd ever had, and Julie warmed up again to this fatherless girl, and felt that Lex was returning some of that warmth, too. Dirk sat back and smiled as if in total approval.

Next day Julie arrived with plenty of time to spend, and watched Dirk riding Soul-searching. The big brown horse was making progress, though slowly, and had his good days and his bad. Dirk, abandoning all tries at jumping him for the present, was working with him on the flat and trying hard to improve the horse's overall attitude toward doing any kind of work whatever.

As always, Julie was fascinated by everything that Dirk did on horseback. A few days ago, watching him school his two jumpers, she had paid him an extravagant compliment which was saved from absurdity only by its sincereness. "You are *fluid,* and you always look in such harmony with the horse! Why, you never get left or have your horse jump out from under you, or put in an extra stride or do any of the things that'd make for a bad fence! You're like a centaur!"

Dirk had laughed, and told her that those things happened to him frequently, but that she was so intent on watching the horse that she missed the finer points of what was happening to the rider.

Most times she'd watched him, though, she'd been up on Cache; today her vantage point was on the ground, and something kept diverting her attention from Dirk to Soul-searching. She could not at first determine what it was. At last she called to Dirk to trot straight toward her, then away from her, then past her.

"Dirk, I think that he's off in the left fore. Only a little, but—yes, I'm sure, he's off."

The young man got off at once and inspected the horse's left leg from elbow to hoof. "Can't feel anything. You're always right, though; I'll have him X-rayed."

"No, don't take my word for it, you watch him." She swung up and jogged Soul-searching on the straightaway. Then she jogged him in a circle to the right, then to the left.

"Yes," Dirk said, "when he has to turn left, for a step or two he's decidedly short. I'll walk him to the barn and call the vet here for a complete set of X rays of both feet." The right foot would be used for comparison, because they had no idea what they might find.

"Incidentally, Julie, this is Lex's saddle I've been riding. Lex volunteered it so mine would be clean for you to use. I think you're bringing her out of her shell," said Dirk, a cautious hope in his voice. "You're what she's needed, a friend she can talk to besides me."

"I do hope so," said Julie, making a mental note that it had been thoughtful of Lex, and she'd have to thank her.

They tacked Cache with Dirk's saddle, and Julie asked where Alexis was. "She was around a little while ago, while I was getting poor old Soul together, but I think she said something about going into Meriden."

They went out of the barn and Julie mounted from the ground, then rode out to the ring. She was feeling the new saddle out; it was so much flatter than her own that it took some getting used to. "I keep realizing that there's nothing in front of me," she told Dirk as she trotted by him. But after a quarter hour of working around on the flat, she began to like the feel of it. "It's more like a racing saddle that anything else I've ridden," she said. "Can I jump a couple of fences in it?"

"I think not."

"Oh, I'll pester till you agree! How can I judge it properly if I don't try everything?"

"I'm not sure that you ought to try jumping in such a drastically different saddle till you're more sure of yourself in it."

"You think I'm still tense about that dumb fall I took? Dirk Markham, I've been falling off horses all my life! Don't you cluck and brood over me any more!"

"All right. I'll lower one of Lex's fences, and you jog down to it and see how it feels."

She trotted to the fence half a dozen times without mishap, increasingly delighted with the saddle. "I really feel so much more with it! Why didn't you have me try it weeks ago? I mean, the whole spectrum of jumping from take-off to landing is right underneath me. Almost touching. I love your saddle, and I don't need to try any others, this is *it*. I'm going to order one this afternoon!" She cocked her head at him. "I would like to try a couple of cantering fences."

"It won't make much difference in the feel of it."

"Couldn't I take just a few?"

"You're dying to do it, so I may as well acquiesce with a good grace," said Dirk. He was shaking his head and smiling ruefully, plainly considering himself a softie where she was concerned. "I'll set up two fences at three-feet-three." He did so. "Now this will ride in a steady four," he told her; that meant that it would be a steady four strides between the pair of fences. "Instead of sitting down after the first jump, land and stay in your half-seat and feel for the rhythm: one, two, three, four, and he'll leave the ground."

"Right," said Julie, squirming with eagerness.

She rode back, headed Cache at the little brush-and-rail fence, met it just right, landed in perfect balance, and steadied for the four anticipated strides to the wall-and-rail spread. "One . . . two . . . three . . . fo—"

She never finished the count in her head, for as Cache pushed off for the spread fence, she felt with a surge of panic that her right leg was unaccountably giving way, dropping into space. . . . With a shrill yip of astonishment, she lurched crazily forward and to her right, fell endlessly through space for seconds that seemed hours, and smacked the earth abruptly on the far side of the wall.

The horse, who had been jerked sharply in the mouth as his rider fell, became wholly confused in mid-air and, unnerved and unbalanced, hurled himself into the midst of the rails and brought everything crashing to the ground, though by chance he himself was quite unhurt and managed to stay upright. As Julie tried desperately to haul herself out of the ruin, the final rail, balanced teetering atop the wall where it had fallen from its standard, was jarred loose and fell with a thump directly on her left foot. She howled shamelessly and dragged herself out from under the wreckage.

Dirk had caught Cache and raced back to Julie's side.

"What happened?" she asked, dazed and confounded. "There suddenly just wasn't anything there, under my right foot!"

"The stirrup leather broke. I don't get it," said Dirk, sounding nonplussed. "I'm sure it was okay when I cleaned it yesterday. And you don't have that heavy a foot, honey —how are you?"

She got to her feet and immediately sat down again. "I wrenched my stupid ankle, I think," she said between gritted teeth. "I'll ride him back if you put me aboard, though."

He looked at her ankle. "It's swelling already. You won't be riding anyplace." In spite of her protests, he handed her the reins to Cache's bridle and scooped her up into his arms to carry her to the barn, the gray trailing behind at the end of his lead. The ankle hurt, throbbing and shooting pain up her leg.

"I'm having a run of miserable luck these days," she said, trying to sound cheerful about it.

Without answering, Dirk immersed her foot in a tub of cold water. Then he said, "Don't budge. Not one muscle.

I'll put Cache away. Then I'll run you to the hospital in Cochranville for X rays."

"Oh no you will not!" she shouted. "I've had far worse falls off race horses, Dirk! I will under no conditions waste your time and mine with any such idiocy! This thing's only wrenched a little. I know the feel of broken bones. Don't be a damp noodle," she finished, subsiding into the cold water once more. "I'm no china doll. I'm not even a thoroughbred."

"You're a tough old buzzard."

"Right. Did you look at that stirrup leather?"

"Yes. It had evidently been pulled thin and then snapped when you were putting your weight on it. No mystery there. Not like—"

"Not like the misplaced fence."

"I was going to say that, yes." He eyed her steadily. "Never expected to ask a mere infant a question like this in cold sobriety, but . . . Julie, do you think Croydon is jinxed?"

"There's no such critter as a jinx."

"The mismeasured obstacle. The broken leather. And don't tell me blithely that my study window shattered in that storm with nothing to help it along, because it's pro- tected by the porch roof and it wasn't exactly thin glass, whatever you're hiding from me."

"That has nothing whatever to do with this ankle."

"I wish I were as sure of that," said Dirk slowly, "as you're pretending to be, my dear girl."

"Are you trying to scare me away from Croydon?"

He looked shocked. "That's the *last* thing I want to happen!"

"Then just forget it. Accidents happen. That's that."

"All right. Dry your hoof and I'll take you home. You have to go to bed as soon as possible. We'll leave your car here for a later trip to Fieldstone—Lex and I will visit tomorrow and bring it then."

On their way to Fieldstone, she thought long and hard, and then told Dirk with resignation, while her ankle beat like a gigantic pulse, "The only way to prevent falling off horses is never to ride them, and it's silly to fuss over it."

"Well, yes. But I'm sorry it had to be *my* saddle you fell from, and none of it your fault. You were doing marvelously."

"I was, wasn't I?" she said complacently. "I'll be back in the saddle before you can say 'Ghosts and goblins!' Oops, sorry."

"It's okay. I'm pondering 'ghosts and goblins' myself," said Dirk darkly.

When Monty heard all about the accident, he asked only one question again. "Why were you riding Dirk's saddle and not your own?"

"Because Dirk wanted me to try it. He wanted me to have more feel of the horse. He thought I'd do better with his leather."

Monty growled, "You did better. You did dramatically better."

"I know what you're thinking, and you're crazy."

"If you know without me saying it, then you must be a little cuckoo yourself, mustn't you?" he asked, and turned on his heel and stamped out of the room, looking like a tall thundercloud heading somewhere to storm all over someone.

Chapter 12

For two days she stayed in bed, fuming and complaining to her dogs about the forced idleness, sweet as honey to Monty and her other human friends. Then she received a present from Stash: an old pair of crutches that his son Beau had had to use once with a broken leg. Overjoyed, she hobbled up and down her cottage until she was used to them and then swung gamely down to the paddock to visit Bonnie.

After gumdrops and sugar lumps and a large carrot for nutritional value, Julie embraced her great mare and made up for the days of neglect with huggings and endearing murmurs. The foals frisked round her, and little Tam asked plaintively for her bottle, with a sudden memory of earlier days.

"Oh, Bonnie," said the girl, "I may be having a lot of fun—and a lot of accidents—with show horses, but you *know* I love you best!"

Bonnie said that she knew.

Dirk and Lex came over the field toward them. This was their third visit in as many days, and Julie was pleased to see Dirk pull out a handful of gumdrops for her mare. "You remembered."

"We did. Hey, you've got crutches! Pieces of eight and fetch aft the rum, we'll have to get you a parrot!" exclaimed Dirk.

"How's the ankle?" asked Lex, always the more practical.

"Miserable, but I guess it's coming along. I can't walk without the crutches, or ride at all, for a week or ten days, Doc says."

"So you gave in and saw a doctor?" asked Dirk.

"Doc Haffner," said Julie, grinning. "Our vet."

Dirk rolled his eyes upward. "About Cache, then."

"Could you—would it be too big an imposition to ask you to work with him?"

"Delighted. I'll begin today. Would have offered myself, but didn't want you to think I was butting in."

"I'll work with him too," said Alexis suddenly, watching her brother.

"I'd certainly appreciate it," said Julie fervently. "You're such sweet people!"

Monty, when he heard of this visit, was not too keen about it, but decided that the less he said about Dirk Markham, the better. And Julie remembered later that she hadn't even asked about Soul-searching, and felt mean and selfish and coldhearted and all sorts of terrible things until they came back next day, to locate her finally in the mare barn. Then she poured out the questions about Soul so fast that neither Markham could manage a word for half a minute.

The news explained many things, and to Dirk's and then to Julie's immense satisfaction. The vet had X-rayed both legs and in the left forefoot had discovered a shadowy area which he believed to be an old, walled-off abscess located almost dead center. This, then, accounted for Soul's awful behavior at the track, and his subsequent, seemingly purposeless fits of frightening activity and bucking explosions. His wilfulness in the gate had undoubtedly come about because as an old hand at the track, and he *had* won some races before going bad, he knew that racing begins at the starting gate, and figured that if he never entered one, he wouldn't have to run. Because the bad foot was his left, he had bolted at the turns, for most horses switch leads and bring all their weight to bear on the inside leg in order to make a turn; and Soul, knowing that the pain would be there, had simply borne out.

The only thing the abscess didn't explain was his attempt to jump the rail; but then, horses do strange things when in the grip of panic.

The treatment prescribed hot-water soaks as often as could be managed, and then having Soul done up in hot poultices for the stretch from evening to morning.

"Since I've got a bad left foot too, I'll take on the soak-ing-tub minding for an hour or so whenever I'm there," said Julie, "and compensate you a little for schooling Cache. There's only one thing I don't understand—"

"I do," said Stash, who had been listening to their talk. "You're thinkin', why'd a model horseman like Mr. Mark-ham here miss seeing that bad foot before? Same reason his first owner didn't, and *he,*" said Stash, putting an ever-so-gentle emphasis on this, "was a racetrack man, too. Reason is, with an abscess, there's gonna be a cer-tain amount of shiftin' of it around inside the foot. See, Julie? It won't hurt him all the time, and then there's minutes when the pain will be really bad. Maybe only for a stride or two. The horse, he gets to know that that foot's gonna stab him anytime, anywhere, without any warning, and that sours his disposition. Guess it didn't with yours, Mr. Markham, so he must be some kind of superior horse. Only hit him now and then that he's gonna have pain and he don't know why, and so he turns rogue, but just on a temporary basis. Not bein' constant, it would have been hard to detect, see?"

"Only Julie's careful scrutiny at the right moment led to us finding out the facts," nodded Dirk. "I thank my lucky stars that you were there that day, or we might never have discovered what was wrong, and he might have proved so unruly that eventually I'd have had to put him down, never dreaming that he had a legitimate reason for his bad acting."

"Horse always has a reason," said Stash positively. "It's people are the ones who can't always figure out what it is."

So for some days Julie drove over to Croydon—she could manage the car now—and hobbled around on her crutches and watched Dirk school Cache and minded Soul-searching in his soaking tub. She discovered that the big brown horse had quite a personality, and was as like-able as Cache himself. He made friends with Pushy (Nana stayed home these days) and took to nibbling Julie's ear to ask for sugar every five minutes.

And then one day, just when she was off her crutches and thinking that now everything would be fine, the *next* thing happened. And it would not have happened—as so many unsettling and important and unexpected things would not have been happening in the past sixteen months or so—had it not been for Nana.

Nana had been good for ages. Nana had been a gem, a jewel, a marvel of obedient domesticity. So Julie relented when the beagle whimpered and rolled her eyes, and Julie took the beagle to Croydon with her. After some dubious moments, Julie removed the leash from the beagle, and the beagle wandered off brightly, tail wagging furiously, in search of mischief and trouble. All the time, of course, looking extremely responsible.

Dirk led Cache out of the stable and greeted Julie as though he hadn't seen her in weeks. "How's Cache coming?" she asked.

"He's a handy jumper. He really is very clever. You've seen how he looks for his own spot in front of a fence? He's doing it all on his own; I'm not helping him a bit. Anywhere within striking distance is all right with him, but still he isn't growing careless about it, which a lot of horses tend to do. Maybe his crashes have made him realize that he can get hurt if he doesn't pay attention. He's becoming more fence-wise by the day. By the time you step back on him, he'll be telling you what to do."

That would be just fine with Julie; the more experienced Cache became, the easier she'd feel about riding him over fences. Dirk went out to the right and took a line of them on Cache and it was lovely to watch, with no errors in judgment by either man or horse, no tight situations, never a take-off from an impossible place, or 'burying' of the horse at the base of a fence with barely enough room for him to fold his knees and get his legs clear of the obstacle. . . . She envied Dirk his easy familiarity with the ways of jumping horses and riding to fences, but she knew that, as he said, when she'd been doing it as long as he had, she'd be at least as good as Dirk.

She was perched on the stone-wall jump. Dirk was coming down the line of fences again. And suddenly there was Nana in full pursuit of a rabbit, streaking directly across Cache's path in front of a fence. "Oh, NO!" The cry was wrenched out of a girl who had just realized at last, through and through, that her beagle was incapable of being reformed and that there was real danger out there at this instant for horse and rider.

Since the gray was already committed to leaving the ground, there was nothing he could do to avoid hitting the dog except change his direction in flight. This would not have been too difficult for an experienced mount, but poor Cache was still quite green; in his effort to miss the rocketing beagle, who was as always oblivious to the trouble she was causing, he hooked a foreleg between two rails. Somehow he kept his balance, but came to a halt a few steps away, shuddering and throwing up his head with shock and pain.

Julie was on her way, limping as fast as her foot would allow, and Dirk was out of the saddle and steadying Cache with hands and words.

The horse had peeled the hide off his tendon as though it had been a banana; it was not spurting blood, but was raw and red and smartly bruised. Julie realized that it must be washed clean and bandaged at once to keep the flies and dirt out.

"That fool dog!" she snapped out. "She goes on a leash till she's thirty years old now! We need some Furacin, Dirk," mentioning her favorite ointment, a bright yellow panacea that she swore by.

He thought, examining the wound. "Haven't got any, but there's some pink ointment that'll do as well. It's also an antibiotic. I have it in the stable—no, by gosh, it's at the house. I'll run for it, Julie; you see to Cache."

"Okay. Come on, fellow, the lame will get the halt home safe, you'll see." Julie led him slowly to the barn. "You wish you'd never seen this place by now, don't you?" she asked him. "The groceries and attention sure don't make up for all your misfortunes. I hope this doesn't . . ." then she stopped, afraid that if she voiced her fear, he would somehow understand, and become so leery of jumping that he would be spoiled for the profession she'd chosen for him.

Julie *knew* that horses do not comprehend English, but there was always that small, childish, clinging doubt deep within her eternally young heart.

She washed the leg with tincture of green soap, being careful not to scrub too hard lest she really make it bleed. Cache stood patient and noble, looking off into space and occasionally sighing like a human casualty. Julie was drying the wound with a clean cloth when Lex came in with a jar of pink ointment. "Oh, I'm so sorry, Julie. He's had more than his share of hard luck here at Croydon, hasn't he?"

"Nobody's fault, Lex."

"Unless—"

"Unless what?"

"Oh, dear," said Alexis, frowning, "never mind. It's those old stories. Sometimes they get to me. And once or twice I've . . . you wouldn't tell Dirk?"

"No, what?"

"I've thought I've seen things around the house where there shouldn't have been anything."

"You aren't crazy," Julie said firmly, "because I have too."

"It's as though something were out to get you. You or Dirk."

"Dirk? He hasn't been hurt."

"No, but he came close to it today, didn't he?"

"Oh wow, yes he did," said Julie. "But what ghost, if it was a ghost, would want to hurt a horse?"

"I don't know. To get rid of all of us, maybe. To have the farm back again to itself. Or themselves."

"That's too weird to think about! How do I use this ointment, just like Furacin?"

"This is Morusan. It works wonders. I've had wonderful luck with it. Don't worry," said Lex, inspecting the horse's leg, "this will be healed in a few days, and the ointment will keep it soft so it won't draw and be stiff. Rub it in well, then run a bandage over it. I'll get one from the cabinet."

Julie thought heavily as she rubbed in the pink goo. When Lex came back the blonde girl said, "This has been a year for leg injuries, that's for sure! First Pushy, then Soul-searching—'course that was an old one, but we just found it—and me, and now Cache."

"What happened to Pushy?"

"He had a cut paw."

"Oh, how'd he get that?" asked Lex.

"Come to think of it, I don't know! I was so busy with Bonnie and the twins I forgot to check. But he stepped on glass or something sharp. He was shut in my cottage, but he got out somehow and first thing I knew there he was, bleeding all over me."

"You didn't find whatever it was?"

"Nary a sign of it. I'd forgotten about it because he's all better now. But with Soul and Cache and me . . . well, it's spooky."

"I don't like it," said Alexis. "I don't like this place much any more, either. I think we ought to leave it to its former tenants."

"You mustn't give up like that. *I* think—"

She was rolling on the bandage, and looked up at a sharp throat-clearing from Lex to see Dirk come into the barn. He said, "All okay?"

"Good as can be with a scrape like that, poor old fellow," said Lex.

"You put on the Morusan?"

"No," said Lex caustically, "we ate it."

"That phone call," he went on, wincing at her sarcasm, "are you sure you had the number right? I called, but there wasn't any Mr. Gisborne there."

"Well, I could swear I heard him clearly; he'll call back if it's as important as he sounded."

When Julie had finished with her gray invalid, it was nearly three, and she hurried home for her Bonnie-time at Fieldstone and her chores, which she could manage now despite the residual limp. Just as she was thinking of bed, her phone rang. It was Dirk.

"Hey, you got a telephone in after all?"

"Yes, yesterday. Don't you remember, I had a call today?"

"Oh, that's right. Did he call back?"

"No. Likely a wrong number. Julie, I don't know quite how to tell you this—"

"Just tell me," she said, growing cold at the worry in his voice.

"Are you sure you used the pink ointment and nothing else?"

"Certainly! Why?"

"I just went to the barn for the last time and Cache was stamping and pawing around the stall. I thought the bandage was too tight for him, and pulled him out to reset it. Cache's leg had swollen badly, and blisters were forming. I can't imagine how it happened," he said, sounding as though he were chewing his lip, "but something's blistered him good and proper."

"Oh, poor Cache!" she wailed. "I'll be right over."

"No, no, that's impractical and unnecessary, dear. I've fixed him up as far as anyone can and the vet's on the way to double-check. Come over in the morning if you can."

"First thing," said Julie.

First thing to Julie was a quarter to seven, and she walked into the empty barn to see Cache. Dirk had not exaggerated. The leg was puffed like a hideous balloon from forearm to coronet. Her poor horse! She was petting him, and he was responding sluggishly to the affection, when Dirk entered.

"Heard your car when you passed the house. Don't worry about Cache looking drowsy, the vet doped him up against the pain. Julie, tell me exactly what you did yesterday, will you?"

She repeated the procedure. Dirk went to look for the jar of ointment. "It isn't here."

"I think I almost finished it."

"That's right, Lex was going in to the Tack Shop to get another jar. Well, there's no replacement here, I suppose they didn't have Morusan; but there's a brand-new jar of Furacin." He returned. "If I weren't a hundred percent certain that I'd sent you the right stuff, I'd swear you'd put a merc-oxide blister on this horse! Heaven knows that's the last thing you'd use on an open wound, much less bandage over it."

"Will he be all right?"

"The vet says yes."

"Whew," said Julie. "When?"

"Six weeks, longer. I'd say it would be at least that long before the leg shrinks back to normal, and in doing so, forms the scurf." This would be the scabby crust that forms after a blister. "When that sloughs off, and after he's thoroughly recovered, we'll start him again. But it's a long time to be away from the course, and naturally he can't be ridden at all until then."

"I guess that means—" Julie began ruefully.

"No, it doesn't. You can practice jumping whenever you like on my open jumper, you're up to him now; and when the fox hunting begins, I'll expect you to be up on Dragonhold as we planned."

"I never planned on Dragonhold! She's your best field hunter."

"Didn't I mention it before? She's your mount for the hunts, and I won't take a no on that. Now suppose we take poor Cache here and van him over to Fieldstone while he's still drowsy enough to be docile about it."

Alexis came out of the shadows of the barn. "I'll drive the van, Dirk. You have more work to do here than I do, and Julie and I never see enough of each other."

Dirk stared at her. "Why, that would be kind of you, Lex," he said, and looked pleased, not to say baffled by her offer.

They loaded the crippled gray in the van and secured him as comfortably and safely as possible. Julie said a hasty goodbye to Dirk and hopped in as Lex got the big vehicle under way. "Your horse isn't all that happened last night," said the girl with the fine-boned and beautiful face. "I mean, what happened to him was followed by what happened to me."

"*More?*" demanded Julie.

"You won't tell Dirk?"

Julie wrestled briefly with loyalties. "Okay, I won't. If you don't think he ought to know."

"He couldn't do anything about it, and he's worried enough about your accidents and Cache. Well, I woke up last night and felt something in my room."

"You mean you heard something, or what?"

"No, just felt that I wasn't alone. And after a minute, when I was getting creepy sensations and thinking about shouting for Dirk, there was a crash across the room. I clicked on my bedlamp right away, and I was alone after all. But," said Lex, and Julie saw a shudder run through her, "my big alabaster owl had fallen off a perfectly level table and shattered on the floor. And I always kept him at least a foot from the edge of the table."

"Did you look under the bed?" asked Julie, slightly incredulous.

"And in both closets. Nothing. And I loved that owl . . . I'm afraid I told Dirk I knocked him over accidentally."

Julie thought. "Yes," she said at last, "if it could have been a prowler, then he'd have to know. But when it couldn't have been anything we understand, I guess you're right not to fret him."

They chewed it over between them all the way to Fieldstone, offering explanations and demolishing them. Lex, who proved knowledgeable in the field, said that when skeptics couldn't explain away ghosts they attributed their sounds and acts to underground rivers, currents of air, earth tremors, swamp gas, and just about anything that couldn't be checked out. "But nothing short of an earthquake could knock over a fifteen-pound statue," she said positively, "and, well, Julie, I just don't much like Croydon!"

"Things will work out," said Julie uneasily, "you just wait and see."

"I have to," said Lex, "I live there, I have no other place to go. But if *I* lived on Fieldstone—catch me within a mile of Croydon then!"

They put Cache into his old stall and Lex said goodbye. Stash and Leon, then Monty arrived, and listened to Julie and examined the gray. They all concurred with the six-weeks diagnosis.

"Who told you to treat his leg the way you did?" Monty asked.

"Dirk, of course." She turned and stared at him. "Are you suggesting what you've been hinting at every time I get a scratch? That Dirk's behind it? Do you think that man would hurt a *horse?*"

She had never been really angry with Monty in her life before. Peeved, yes, snitted, provoked, but not angry. This was Monty Everett. But he persisted.

"How did that fence misplace itself? Why were you riding a saddle with a stirrup leather that was ready to snap? Who told you to put what must have been a pink mercuric oxide blister on an open sore?"

"Who put the glass axe in your kitchen?" Stash nodded, and caught himself and looked guiltily over at Leon.

"What are you all talking about?"

"What glass axe?" said Monty.

"Thing Pushy stepped on and cut himself. Little old glass hatchet from Washington's Birthday or something."

"I didn't have any glass hatchet," said Julie blankly.

"We know that," said Leon, taking command in his calm fashion, "but it was there, and it got broken, and Pushy cut himself on a piece. Stash and me, we figured it was someone tryin' to scare you away from the Croydon place. It suggested Croydon."

"Why? How?"

"It was an axe, and there was blood-red paint on the blade, and that means Croydon around here."

"Oh, dear," said Julie, and recovered and launched out again. "But Dirk, oh no, not Dirk! He'd die before he hurt an animal, and I know that as well as I know it about all three of you. And not Lex either, she lives and breathes horses. And she's scared too."

"Of what? Something's been happening to her?" asked Leon.

"Yes. Little, dumb things. No sense to them. No reason at all. She wants to get away from the place. Well," said Julie, inhaling and stabbing her finger at them one by one, "whatever, whoever it is, it is not Dirk Markham, and I won't stand here and listen to innuendoes about him." She shook her head. "Besides, if he wanted to scare me off Croydon, he wouldn't have to! He could just say I wasn't welcome. But he begs me to come oftener!"

"And does Alexis?"

"No. But she's friendly now and confides in me, and she's scared, I tell you."

"A glass axe falls, and Pushy's hurt. A fence moves, and you come a cropper. I forgot—you go to feed the Croydon stock, and—"

"And Dirk makes it storm, and causes the wind to slam the door," said Julie scornfully.

"Okay, forget that part. But he persuades you to use his saddle, which collapses under you. And he gives you a pink ointment that lays up a good horse for six weeks or better," finished Monty doggedly. "Explain all that, leaving out any possibility of Dirk's being out to hurt you for some crazy purpose of . . ."

He stared at Leon, whose face had undergone a remarkable change. Leon said, "Stash, you done any more detective work on the Markhams?"

"Some. Hard to find out things about 'em. Stepbrother and stepsister, orphaned, came from near Cochranville, disappeared twelve-thirteen years ago, came back this year to buy Croydon. But no old pals left around here that they've visited, it seems. Nobody to look up and talk about old days—all the kids he knew, they're gone, some to the army, some to other places. So that leaves one thing mighty hard to check out."

"What?" asked Leon, as though he already knew the answer.

"Whether Dirk Markham really is Dirk Markham. That's all."

"Well, who else could he *be?*" said Julie, shrill.

Monty said, "I see the way your notion's leaning, Stash,

and yours too, Leon, and I feel cold along the spine. Who?"

"I can't say who, doggone it! I can only say that I tried to find out if the Croydon boy is still in that institution, and I couldn't. The age is about right."

"You mean the boy who m-murdered his foster parents?" asked Julie thinly.

"Yes. I'm not even hintin' that Dirk is Croydon, mind. I'm only saying what I did and didn't find out. No asylum's gonna answer questions about an inmate when they're bein' asked by a nobody groom from Fieldstone who isn't related to that inmate. Nobody around has heard he was let out, but that doesn't signify. People have moved, forgot, or turned their backs on the whole memory. But one thing, to be fair: Markham needed a pile of money to build up his stable and buy the farm and all, and he dresses like money from way back; and the Markhams they were well-to-do, and the Croydon boy wouldn't own much more'n the shirt on his back, because his folks had sunk most of their earnings right back into that farm while they were alive. So I'd say, barrin' further developments, that Markham is Markham. But why would he want to hurt Julie or her horse?"

"Or his sister?" Julie supplemented. "He wouldn't. He loves both of us—"

"Oh?" said Monty, crescendo.

"As much as he loves his own horses, and Cache, and even ornery little Nana! So this whole conversation," said Julie Jefferson, "is too idiotic to be withstood a minute longer!" And she stamped off to do her chores.

The three men stood silently with the injured horse, thinking their own thoughts. At last Leon said, "Stash?"

"Yes?"

"Keep on digging."

"Right."

"Too many accidents make a reason behind them. And ghosts, from what I understand, don't mess around with ointment, saddles, fences, or glass hatchets. So you dig." He turned to Monty. "You going back to the track anyways soon?"

"No," said Monty, "I just decided that I really need a longer rest. I'll be around, Leon."

"Good," said the foreman and the groom together.

Chapter 13

Any suspicion of Dirk that had ever whispered in her ear had long since died away and been forgotten, and Julie in the days that followed visited Croydon freely, though not so often now that Cache was not there. Dirk lectured her and demonstrated and watched her work, and pronounced her, though still slightly lame, fit for the first fox hunt of the year. Overjoyed, she rushed home to tell Monty, who was almost as enthusiastic about the whole business as he would have been if she'd told him she was going to swim the Mississippi lengthwise.

He found it hard not to protest. But he mused glumly that he couldn't *order* her not to go, or accuse a man point-blank of being a lunatic and murderer, on the strength of a couple of slight accidents and an ointment that had burned a horse. By this time, in fact, Monty was so confused that he wasn't sure it had been the ointment. He didn't even know what he thought, he told himself lamely, and said, "Good luck, and I'm glad it'll be a drag you're following and not some poor doomed fox," and shut up.

The Saturday of the meet, Julie arrived at Croydon an hour early. She had hoped to see Lex alone, since they'd had almost no chance to talk and the younger girl had been looking rather hollow-eyed and sleepless lately; but she was in the stable, while Dirk was on the porch and called jovially to Julie to come in while he finished his own preparations, and they'd walk to the stable together.

She found herself waiting in the study, where she had been so terrified that stormy night. She walked around, noting that the floor had been professionally sanded and the stains had faded to a ghost—no, a shadow—of their previous horror. There were still no rugs laid; Dirk had said that they were on the way, along with the rest of the Markhams' furniture.

Julie wandered about, peeking into things as was her habit—not private things, like desk drawers, of course, but up the chimney and in bookcases. She noticed that the sun, striking in low from just above the horizon to the east, showed a slightly raised board by the hearthstone; the sanding machines had either lifted it or by cleaning away the accumulation of years had disclosed the fact that it sat higher than its neighbors. After a longish wait, and without a thought in her head except that anything even a jot out of place in an old house like this . . . 1935, after all, maybe they'd still been constructing hidden staircases and secret chambers . . . was worth investigation, she knelt and edged her fingertips along the side of the board. It was not exactly loose, but it did move a fraction of an inch upward.

Julie pushed her fingers down tighter and shoved. The board lifted, so that she could see where it had rested on the ends of a couple of two-by-fours. In the dark recess below, she caught the dull glint of metal. Excited now, she raised the board farther.

The long-handled axe lay there, threatening and terrible in its immobility. The dust of the years did not hide the thick, dark old stains on blade and handle. With a muffled squeal, Julie dropped the board into place and stamped on it, as though the awful thing might rise and come up after her under its own power. It was the most horrible sight her young eyes had ever seen. She knew instantly what it was, she could almost see it being hidden there— how long ago?—thirteen years or more. This had been the weapon that had killed those two good and harmless people.

Let sleeping madness lie! She trampled on the board along its length until it seemed to be level with the rest of the floor.

Why in the world hadn't the police found the horrid thing? It was hidden in so obvious a place. Perhaps the rug that had lain here originally was a big one, and had cov-

ered the floor with no sign of ever being pulled up. Should
she tell Dirk? There was an urge in her to share the secret
and lessen its terror for herself. . . .

No. No sense in peopling his new home with more
tangible nightmares than haunted it now. His rugs would
soon cover it forever. She hoped that he, and especially
Alexis, would never make the same discovery that she
had.

And perhaps it wasn't there at all. She could still see it
in her mind's eye, but she was well aware that she had a
most vivid imagination. Or maybe it was only the ghost
of an axe. Oh, *stupid!* It lay there, all right. Let it lie.

"Poking around, Julie?" said Dirk, coming abruptly into
the study. "Finding interesting things, I hope?"

"No! I mean, yes, I love your brooks. Your books.
And the furniture's lovely. I wasn't prying, really," she
said with a surge of something akin to dread, as his large
blue eyes rested on her face unwaveringly. "Just fiddling
around."

"Great Scott, browse all you like! This is almost your
home too, you know."

"Yes. Oh. Ready?" she asked, as brightly as she could
manage.

"Yes, and you?"

"Yes indeed," she said, and scuttled past him to the
front door.

"You *are* in a rush to follow the hounds, aren't you?"
said Dirk, sounding amused.

"I sure am," said Julie, endeavoring to forget her find
and to concentrate on the exciting time ahead. "Are you
certain you want me to have Dragonhold instead of you?"

"She's best for you, the most experienced and steadiest.
And she likes you. Not that all the horses don't! But as
Master of the hunt, and Huntsman too, I'll be perfectly
well mounted on Pootle. Lex, of course, will be riding On
Target."

The day was mild and damp, and Dirk said that this
was good, because the scent of the drag would lie well.
They tacked up and the three of them jogged to where the
hounds and the riders and horses were assembled, some

four or five minutes from the main buildings of Croydon. The hounds were just being let out of the pick-up truck that had brought them here; it had a built-up rear end to contain them and resembled a camper. The two whippers-in were moving among them, squeaking quietly to them as they waited for Dirk.

"I ought to have been here before this," he told Julie as they approached the colorful mob of people and animals. "Well, this isn't a formal meet by any means. The local snobs had a second fit about that, the first one erupting when they heard that we'd follow a drag! But I just want to get the hunt started, and teach you novices something of the etiquette and regulations. Later the hunt will be much more formal, and you'll all have to be outfitted with proper clothing, and kick in for the fence funds, and tip me five dollars if I award you the mask or brush—"

"Just what I always wanted," said Julie, "the mask of a nice well-used drag." She was still nervous, still trying to seem entirely herself when she wasn't. The hidden weapon remained in the background of her mind.

"I'll cast the hounds," Dirk said to the first Whip, and murmured to Julie and Lex, " 'Their minds being memories of smells, their voices like a ring of bells . . .' now comes the pleasure of the thing. Now comes the pack."

One of the dogs gave tongue abruptly. Julie looked her query and Lex, beside her, said, "No, see how the others ignore him? He's a babbler, he talks to hear himself, out of excitement. We'll have to get rid of him."

The hounds quartered back and forth over the ground with mounting enthusiasm. Dirk was gone now, ready to take his place at the head of the field when they should find the scent. The riders, most of whom were local farmers whom Julie knew, with a sprinkling of dolled-up landowners and horse-show people, were all silent now, watching and waiting.

One of the Whips chastised the babbler, who shut up and looked remorseful. "That's called rating the hound," said Lex. "That's the biggest job of the whippers-in, to

keep the hounds in order and make them obey the Huntsman, who never rates them himself."

"Doesn't that crop hurt them?" asked Julie.

"Just startles them. Stings a little. No more than the
bat on a racehorse."

Suddenly a hound, a steady old-timer at the business,
announced the scent, which his delicate and true nose had
picked out of the multitude of other smells that surrounded
him. As he spoke to the others, they massed around him,
and suddenly there came the burst—the first eager run,
often the most scorching pace of the whole hunt, with
"hounds' music" filling the air. The riders streamed away
in pursuit, everyone careful not to pass the Master.

Julie had had her reservations about Dragonhold, who
was a fantastic runner. She'd worried about being able to
hold her in once the fervor of the race had taken hold;
she'd even pictured herself committing the most dreadful
sin of all hunting, riding over the hounds. She needn't
have fretted. The mare was sluggish in her gallop, and
actually began to fall behind the field (which means the
members of a hunt).

"Why are you holding her in?" called Lex, still beside
her.

"I'm not! She's just slow."

"Dragon?" Lex cocked a quizzical eyebrow. "Okay,
I'll have to leave you, then." She shot On Target forward
like a gigantic bullet, and forged up behind Dirk.

"Come on, baby," said Julie, using every skill she knew
to get the mare moving well. Being left behind was the
fate of every novice at least once or twice in his first
season, but this was ridiculous. "Come *on*, Dragon!"

Dragonhold lumbered valiantly along at about the pace
of a good cart horse. The crying of the hounds in their
pursuit grew noticeably farther off, and before the first Fairfield gate had come in sight, Julie had all but lost the field.
She felt like crying. She had seldom been so humiliated.

And yet the mare seemed to be doing her best.

Julie heard the pack ahead and to her left. She took the
Fairfield gate well enough and headed down a lane toward the sound. There were no other riders in sight. She

forded a stream, pounded up a hill, and crested it to see the field stretched out behind the Master while the hounds tore over a meadow in a bugling pack. One of them was skirting—hanging back a little wide, hunting on his own—and a Whip was galloping to head him into the thick of things. It was a beautiful scene, and Julie, crestfallen, would have given almost anything to be a part of it; but she was already a quarter of a mile in the rear.

"This can't be happening to me," she said severely to her mount. "What *is* the matter?"

Dragonhold picked up a morsel of speed.

They went down and across the meadow, hearing the pack in full cry. Julie charged the mare through brush and over a low stone wall and realized that now Dragonhold was running much better. Did it always take her ten minutes to warm up? There was so much country all around, of such varying types, and Julie could work only by ear; if the pack decided to run mute, she'd be totally lost.

There was a water jump ahead. Julie put the mare to it and flew over splendidly into a stubbly field. Abruptly there was a figure, hardly glimpsed in the rush, rising from brush just to her left. Julie had an impression of stiff arms waving from a flapping body, a stark white head under a flopping hat; then she was wholly occupied with a panicked, runaway horse.

Julie had sat on runaways before, and sometimes been thrown and sometimes fallen with the beast, but usually had been able to run it out and eventually calm the horse into control. She was so discredited now in her own eyes, having lost the field in the first few breaths of the hunt, that nothing on earth but Dragonhold crossing her legs and coming a cropper was going to unseat the girl. And nothing did, although the mare was blind with fear and several times would have run straight into fences or under low-hanging boughs if Julie had not turned her by main force. They ran it out together and eventually stood, panting (both of them), on the bank of a stream.

Julie got off and soothed Dragon, fed her some crumbly sugar cubes, and wiped her own streaming face with a handkerchief.

"There, it wasn't your fault. It was that spook," she said. The word jolted her. "What was it? It didn't look—no, it absolutely wasn't human!"

The horse apparently agreed with her.

"Croydon," Julie whispered, her nape generating ripples of chill. "Croydon is . . . is cursed!" She smoothed the damp hair of the horse's neck and shoulder. "Oh, never mind!" she said, irritated with herself and with whatever uncanny thing had frightened her mare, "Where's the hunt gone, d'you suppose?"

She listened hard, and birds called and insects hummed and sang; but either the pack had checked, having lost the scent for the moment, or were running mute. "Or that mad dash carried us out of range," she said to Dragonhold. "Well, let's try to find them."

She mounted and rode out. Then she heard a hound speak in the distance and the others join in, and she turned her horse toward the sound. In five minutes, Dragonhold now going well and as though she'd never been scared in her life, the field came in view.

Shortly she had caught them and from that time on never lost them again. The hunt was heady, the drive and determination of both hounds and horses never flagging, until at last it was over, the "fox" had been run to earth, the hounds rewarded, and the post mortems begun.

Dirk found her in the milling throng of riders. "Where were you all that time? You weren't thrown, were you?"

"No, but almost," she said, and told him of Dragonhold's initial sluggishness, which amazed him, and of the weird figure that had caused the mare to bolt. "I don't know what it was, but it wasn't a person or an animal, I saw that much."

"Let's go back that route, then. The Whips will take care of the dogs." Collecting Alexis, they rode leisurely across country till they came to the stubbly field and the water jump. Julie pointed out the place where the thing had risen, and Dirk, dismounting, searched it thoroughly. "Nothing here," he said, scowling. "Are you dead sure, Julie?"

"No question about it!"

He gave her an odd look. "Well, you came through safe and in the saddle, and that's what counts. But I wish I knew what was going on, I really do."

"No more than I do," said Lex darkly.

"Me too," said Julie Jefferson.

September came, and Bonnie's twins had been weaned with the usual amount of loud horse conversation between foals and dam, and Monty had reluctantly gone back to the track to earn his keep. When her work and her time with Bonnie permitted it, Julie still zipped over to Croydon to practice her jumping, and nothing odd happened for weeks, which, perversely, made her uneasy.

One day Dirk happily showed her where the abscess had finally burst through at Soul-searching's coronet band. Now it was draining, and he hoped to be riding the big fellow within a few days.

"And how's Cache doing?"

Julie was petting Soul, whose disposition had become positively sunny. "He'll make you a wonder horse now, you'll see. . . . Cache? Oh! He's coming along about as everybody predicted. A thick crust of scurf has formed, and Leon says it'll start peeling off after a while."

"And have you decided definitely about Bonnie?" he asked, coming around to Julie's most frequent preoccupation.

"Yes. She's turned out again with the barren mares, and we didn't breed her. We've all agreed that we'll try her at the track for another year before retiring her. In December we'll start to leg her up slowly, and if possible —and it does look possible—we'll start running her in late March or early April."

"I've never laid a bet in my life, but I will when she's out there," said Dirk warmly. "You convinced me long ago that she's the horse of the century."

"She is," said Julie emphatically.

The weather was warm for September, and the mares of Fieldstone Farm were still being turned out at night and kept in during the day; that evening, as usual, Bonnie was put to graze, and Julie said goodnight to her and went home to bed with Nana and Pushy.

Some hours later, about midnight in fact, a figure approached the big mare, who looked up from her grazing at the sound of her name. A hand was held out, and Bonnie snuffled at it and then ate the gumdrops off the palm. Thereafter she submitted to having a halter put on, and with only token resistance followed the human being out of the grazing ground and across to Ogden's Mill Road. Her foals had been weaned for more than two weeks, or Bonnie would never have consented to go anywhere; but she recognized the scent and the voice of this human, and when she was urged into a trailer that sat under some trees by the road, she entered resignedly.

Being secured, she rode for some time and then was led out into the night again, and to a small, long-unused pasture with a run-in shed. There she was left, and after fifteen or twenty minutes of nervously whickering and staring around her at the unfamiliar shapes, Bonnie settled down and began to graze once more.

The trailer had disappeared, along with the human.

There was really no accounting for the actions of the human race.

Chapter 14

"Well, one good thing I can see, that's all," said Stash sadly. "When she found out Bonnie was gone, she hollered for Monty and not for Dirk. He ought to be along any hour now."

"You know what that sheriff said," demanded Leon for the tenth time; "he said that this was honest country and that somebody'd find her and bring her back! Said he'd spread the word! Best mare in the United States and he's gonna 'spread the word'! How you like that for police work?"

"He's got every man available lookin' for her too, you know," Stash objected. "You want him to rush out and arrest all the usual suspects, or what?"

"I've told Mr. T time after time," Leon went on, unheeding. "Hire yourself the Pinkertons, I've told him. You got a million dollars worth of horseflesh on this place, and all the guards you have amount to a nightwatchman who can't be everyplace at once! I told him."

"Nobody stole Bonnie," Stash said. "She wandered off. You saw how that gate—"

"I saw how somebody fixed that gate to look like it hadn't been latched, but Stash Watkins, if you stand there and tell me again how Julie neglected to fasten it, I'm gonna forget your great age and pop you in the eye."

"I never said Julie didn't fasten it. All I know, that fool beagle of hers mighta knocked it loose. What'd you ever go and give her that scatterheaded pup for, anyway?" said Stash, aggrieved. "Been nothing but trouble, and now it goes and lets Bonnie out to run loose."

"Oh, have a peep of common sense, if you can't manage the wisdom of a Kentucky man, you Ohioan," said

149

Leon with scorn. "How does a beagle unlatch a big old gate? I tell you—"

"Don't tell me again, I heard it all forty-six times. Where's Monty, anyhow?" said Stash nervously. "He ought to be here."

"He's a trainer. What we want is detectives and state troopers and bloodhounds!"

"And good old Scotland Yard to the rescue, lickety-split—*hey!*"

"What bit you?" said Leon.

"Scotland Yard! The glass hatchet! Remember us jokin' about Mr. Holmes and all? Wellsir!"

"What do you mean, 'wellsir'? What you talkin' about, Stash?"

"Who we been suspicioning for months of all kinds o' things?"

"Oh, that," said Leon. "Look, I thought of him right off. But he never took Bonnie. He's a bright fellow, he wouldn't take a chance on a grand larceny trial and the rest of his prime in jail. Besides," he added, frowning and glaring as though he dared his friend to object, "Dirk Markham, whatever's been happening over at Croydon since he got there, is all right. I've had my eye on him. He's as horse-folks a man as you're gonna find. No sir, what we want is somebody like those racetrack no-goods that stole Bonnie way back when she was just a yearling."

"You have some sense. What racetrack man's out to steal as well-known a racer as Sunbonnet, Filly o' the Year? What are they gonna do with her? And everybody knows that she broke her leg and can't run, except the people on this very farm that say she will again! So who, in or out of his right mind, would take her? No sir, she wandered off, that's all."

"They could have lifted her to use for a brood mare."

"No way. I don't believe it."

"You don't believe anything that doesn't walk up and step on your foot. I say they ought to be using bloodhounds."

"Well, they likely will! Whole thing only happened

less'n an hour ago." Stash looked at his watch. "Where's Monty?"

"Forty minutes out of Kandahar and breaking the speed laws, that's where." Leon consulted his own timepiece. "What about Julie?"

"She's got Nana and Pushy and half the dogs on the place sniffin' for trails," said Stash. "You know something? I hate to admit you're right, but Mr. T ought to hire about three shifts o' Pinkertons for this place, and Deepwater too. Maybe he will after this. Too easy-going just to figure that because we're out in the sticks nobody's gonna bother us."

"Who you calling a native of the sticks?" shouted Leon.

"You and me, you blame old foreman, you. Simmer down. We got chores to do."

Meanwhile, Pushy, who seemed to have some genuine idea of what his mistress wanted, was snuffling along an apparent scent trail toward Ogden's Mill Road, closely followed by a distraught girl.

Julie had kept her intense desire to scream and weep under firm control, but she could not help the fearful shivering and shaking that convulsed her periodically. It was a nightmare in the worst sense, there was a feeling to it of everything bad that had ever happened to Bonnie returning now, the ghosts of all the crooks and hard characters who'd coveted her thronging about, unseen but felt; and all this mingled with remembered voices in her head, repeating ominously, *Did you see the stirrup leather that broke? You know what a bloody axe means in these parts? Who gave you that ointment? Who measured the fence? What rose out of the brush? Who let the dogs into Croydon House? What broke Lex's owl? Who threw that rock?*

Nobody knows about the dogs and the rock and the phantom figure but me.

Yes, and whoever did it all.

Oh, be quiet! she said inside herself. "Bonnie," she said again to Pushy, whose staunch and intelligent presence did have a soothing effect on her nerves. "Bonnie, Bonnie!" The St. Bernard knew the name, he certainly associated it with Bonnie's scent, and he was following something. There was hope.

Now and then a man would appear on the skyline and vanish again: a groom, an exercise boy, some other employee of Fieldstone; one of the sheriff's men, all of whom, horse-country bred to a man, were very concerned over Bonnie's disappearance. Julie had plenty of help in her search.

If only the great mare, confused by her sudden freedom, had not wandered onto the dangerous highway! But the sheriff had already set up temporary roadblocks a few miles on either side of Fieldstone on Route 143, to warn motorists to drive carefully and to inspect all horse vans and trailers. The back way, too, Ogden's Mill Road, which was now in sight, had been staked out.

I ought to have called Dirk, she thought. Well, somebody will. "Bonnie," she said to Push, "find Bonnie!"

The huge dog came to the road and stopped, looking around him. Roads are so full of harsh odors to dogs that their noses become confused; which is why rabbits will seek out a road and run along it for some distance when pursued by hounds. Pushy started across, halted, cast about, looked at Julie miserably as though to explain that he wasn't equipped for this sort of thing, and then trotted across to a little grove of trees. Here he sat down and sighed lugubriously.

Julie looked around the countryside, then at the ground. A heavy vehicle had been parked here recently. Its tracks came onto the soft ground and then went onto the road again.

A horse van? It was possible.

"Then Bonnie's been kidnapped!" she exclaimed in horror.

"If Pushy's nose is doin' its duty, then you're right," said Stash when she told him. "You got to remember, though, he's no beagle."

"I know, it could be coincidence. Any news at all?"

"Well, Leon phoned in 'Lost' ads to the two papers, Meriden and Cochranville. Monty'll be here any minute now. Everybody that's out on the search has a halter and a pocketful of gumdrops. Man's on his way with two bloodhounds, they'll want to smell her stall good and then go out to where she was last seen."

"Last seen," said Julie mournfully.

"Oh, don't you worry, she'll turn up!" Stash, attempting to be hopeful, sounded like a mourner at a wake. "She's just, well, lookin' for her foals or something."

"She'd be with them now if that was true, Stash. Dear Stash, don't try so hard . . . but thanks, anyway."

"She's been missin' before. We'll find her. This will be the absolute final time, too—Leon talked to the boss, and he's on his way from New York, and he's gonna hire guards, more of 'em than Fieldstone and Deepwater ever saw, because we can't just stand around unprotected any more."

"We'll shut the barn door good and tight," said Julie, "since the horse has been stolen. If I'd had any idea, I'd have slept in the field with her!"

"Shoo," said Stash unhappily.

They walked out into a rising wind. Monty was running toward them from his car. There was a babble of questions and answers and self-accusations and denials and prayerful statements without foundation, and then the bloodhounds arrived and Julie went off with them to show their keeper where the trail had been picked up and ended.

Monty said to Stash, "What about Markham? Has anyone spoken to him?"

"Not that I know of. Julie hasn't."

"I thought she'd be calling for him first thing."

"He's a good friend," said Stash, picking his words, "but the minute she found Bonnie missing, she hollered for you." He looked at Monty. "You take the advice of an old black man who worked for your daddy before ever you were born?"

"I'll take the advice of the best friend I ever had," said Monty.

"Tell Julie you're in love with her. I know blessed well you never have yet. It's time you did, before she gets confused and links up with the wrong boy."

"I never seem to find the right time to broach the subject," said Monty.

"That's because you never been in love with anyone but the one girl, and you sort of got to takin' her for granted; and then you let her tangle your tongue up for you because she goes on at such a rate about horses, you think she isn't interested in you too. That's not so. She is. But she's as shy as you are and she'll set in and babble when she sees you gettin' serious. Take the bit in your teeth and the reins in a firm grip—wait a second, that makes you both horse and rider, don't it? Anyhow," said Stash, giving his shoulder a heavy squeeze, "set her down when this is over and say something about how you feel. She wants you to. I know it."

"I never knew you to be wrong about anything, Stash. Okay."

"Oh, I been wrong once or twice in my life," said Stash, "but not about this. You'll see. Now let's go find that big old mare Sunbonnet."

The morning passed in mounting fear for Bonnie's safety. The bloodhounds had confirmed Pushy's theory that Bonnie had gone over to the back road and there been put into a vehicle of some kind; most likely, said the sheriff, a trailer. He was taking the case even more seriously now that it seemed to be a matter of "stolen" and not simply "strayed." He had casts made of the tire tracks and began a quiet investigation of the surrounding farms, those that bred horses for any purpose. For he agreed with Leon that such a magnificent mare as Bonnie might have been spirited away with the idea of using her as a brood mare.

"Even though they couldn't advertise her as who she is," he told the Fieldstone crew, "she'd be invaluable as the dam of some fine foals, and we all know that. But it was a stupid stunt to pull, because with the casts of the tires we have, we can identify the trailer like a shot. *And* bloodhounds' evidence is acceptable in court. *And* you can't hide a big bay mare indefinitely, not if you own a thousand acres!"

Monty thought of other stupid stunts then: stunts with

fences and stirrups and blisters. He said to Julie, "You haven't told Dirk she's missing?"

"Not yet. I didn't have the strength to go around telling people and listening to their sympathetic words," she said quietly. "Not even Dirk's. Only ours, the family's."

"Why don't we run over to Croydon, pick up your tack, and I'll break the news? He'll want to help, and after all, if the police come prowling and checking his pastures and his tires, he's going to wonder why he didn't hear it first from you."

"Okay. Why get my tack, though?" She stared at him. "You aren't suspecting Dirk of stealing her?"

"You won't be schooling hunters while Bonnie's missing. And you don't want to do it on the phone, do you?"

"Oh, you're right," said Julie, forgetting that he hadn't answered her second question.

Nana romped up as they were striding toward Monty's car, and as she had been missing for hours and Julie had no time to pop her into the cottage, they scooped her up and deposited her, a little muddy and panting, on the back seat.

Dirk was indeed sympathetic, but in a shocked and yet manly fashion that did not cause Julie's eyes to puddle up. He was optimistic without being overly cheerful about it, and Julie was grateful, and Monty was suspicious but baffled. If this man was an actor, Monty told himself, he was a really fine one.

They had not emerged from the car yet, for Dirk had met them on the driveway. Now he said, "Let's get your tack from the barn; you can have a quick visit with Soul-searching, who seems to miss you." Monty and Julie got out, and Nana jumped after them. "Back in there!" said Monty sternly, but Julie said, "She's too tired to run off," and he let it go.

The wind was blowing hard. Nana stood there sniffing it, little compact body aquiver. She followed the humans a few yards, and halted again. Something familiar spoke to her on that wind. Julie turned and called to her sharply. But Nana shook herself and gathered her weary muscles and shot off over the hill, head up as she followed the breast-high scent.

"That mutt!" roared Monty, out of all his patience.

"No, she's serious," exclaimed Julie. "She's on the trail of more than a rabbit! Didn't you see how beat she was? This must be important!"

"A very important skunk," said Monty. "Let her go, it might do her brains some good if she has to walk home to Fieldstone from here."

"I agree with Julie," said Dirk. Monty scowled dismally at him. "I remember you mentioned once or twice that Nana and Bonnie are close pals. I don't say the pup knows Bonnie's lost, but—no harm in checking, is there?"

"What would Bonnie be doing way over here?" asked Julie rhetorically. "She's never been to Croydon." Then the hope came through the unaccustomed despair. "But it took some powerful urging to get Nana to move like that! Let's follow her."

"Oh, Julie," said a very disgusted racehorse man.

"No, I agree. A brisk trot over the hill wouldn't do any harm," Dirk said. His brows were knitted and Julie thought he was somewhat paler than usual under his heavy tan. "Wait here if you like," he said, and went off at a run.

"Three grown people pursuing a dopey beagle," growled Monty, bringing up the rear as Julie took off like a blond bullet.

Yaps and bays floated back, and they came to the top of the hill and saw Nana disappear over the next; and Monty shrugged and ran. Up hill and down dale . . .

In the unused pasture stood Bonnie, whinnying with pleasure at seeing her doggy stablemate walloping toward her.

"Markham—"

"No," said Dirk, as Monty, black in the face, lifted a fist to shake it at him, "no, not me. But I had the feeling she was here. The minute Nana took off. But not by my hand."

"That's easily said, but—"

"Look," said Dirk grimly, "it was my idea to follow

the dog, wasn't it? The whole business just came together in my mind when she yelped out into the wind like that, and I *knew*."

"Knew that Bonnie was here? That's farfetched, isn't it?"

Julie was embracing her mare thankfully, while Nana sat in a dangerous position under the shifting hoofs and panted with delight. She had not known that Bonnie was missing, of course. She was simply overjoyed to find a friend in an unexpected place, and to see Julie happy.

Dirk said, "There's a halter on that post, Monty. If you'll slip it on her, we can walk her back and you can borrow my trailer to carry her to Fieldstone. I'm sorry for all the worry she's cost you, but we'll clear everything up shortly."

Monty, restraining himself from climbing all over Dirk only by keeping in mind the fact that Julie was there, put the halter on Bonnie. "We'll have to call the sheriff's office from Croydon; he has a dozen men or more out looking for her."

"I'm sure he does. I'm sorry," Dirk said again, and looked it. "Call Leon Pitt, too. I imagine the farm's half crazy with the horse's disappearance."

"Right," said Monty; and he stared at Dirk hard, and a thread of doubt crept into his mind. Markham looked unhappy and stern, but not guilty. . . .

That could be acting. But to what purpose?

The insane need no purpose.

Monty carefully maneuvered himself between Dirk and the girl. "Ready, Julie?"

She turned a tear-stained face toward them. She hadn't heard a word they'd said until now. "What? Oh, yes. Sorry, but a woman's got a right to cry at a time like this, hasn't she?"

Filled with relief, anger, and bewilderment as he was, Monty noted the words. Julie, to his certain knowledge, had never before referred to herself as anything but a girl. Well, today she'd earned the right and privilege for certain, setting her teeth and being as brave or braver than any man. "Yes," he said to her proudly, "a woman does."

Two handkerchiefs were held out to her. She smiled at Dirk, but she took Monty's and wiped the tears dry.

Then they walked back to Croydon, not speaking at all, while Bonnie came behind them on the lead and Nana, tired as an Olympic winner, padded alongside and never even glanced up when a rabbit bounced out of the grass and pounded away in fright.

They came down the last slope and saw the cars parked behind Monty's, and the sheriff and three deputies talking to Alexis in the driveway. One of the men held two plaster casts. They had evidently just arrived. Lex was laughing as she talked to them, waving one hand gaily.

When she saw the little procession coming toward her, with the big bay in tow, she went dead white and dropped her arms at her sides. Dirk went up and took her hand. "Come inside, dear," he said gently. "Come and tell us all about it."

Chapter 15

Julie stabled Bonnie while the sheriff talked with Dirk and Alexis just stood there looking numb with shock. Nana lay down in the stall and went instantly to sleep. Julie kissed her lost-and-found beloved, and ran back to the group.

"Come inside and have coffee," said Dirk, his features frozen into stone. "We'll all hear it out. We must."

"I'm afraid so," said the sheriff. He was a large man with a good face that had a permanent bright-red sunburn. "Tom, you check the trailer tires against the casts."

"No need to do that," said Dirk. "No question about it."

"Have to follow procedure anyway, Mr. Markham. Might be a trial."

"Oh, no!" exclaimed Julie.

"Come in," said Dirk, "please come inside and sit down. My sister's ready to faint." He led her up the steps, while the deputies started toward the barn. They went into the study, which had the most furniture to sit down on, and Dirk brought coffee on a tray. Alexis gripped her cup and drank the hot liquid like milk. "Tell us about it, Lex," said her brother.

"What's there to tell?" Her voice was thin but strong. "I met you, Julie, and I saw Dirk fall for you at first sight. I wasn't going to lose my whole family to some rich race-track kid."

"You talk as if Julie was a predatory female," snapped Monty, who was still shaken with the discovery of the truth.

"I never meant to hurt her seriously, only to scare her away from Croydon. At least," said Alexis after a pause, "I don't believe I meant to kill her."

159

No one spoke.

"So I did all those things. But she wouldn't stay away. So I took her horse, to really worry her. I would have taken the mare back after a while. After Julie'd got used to staying away from Croydon."

"Start at the beginning," said Dirk levelly.

"That would be the glass axe," Monty supplied. Dirk blinked, but did not look away from his sister.

"I took it over to put it in her kitchen and scare her; I knew she'd think of Croydon and the murders. But you," Lex said to Julie, her voice rising, "you're protected by a *real* ghost! I heard it in your house, coming toward me, and I dropped the fool hatchet and ran out; and I heard it again here, in this place, when I was figuring how to spook you good!"

"I don't know what you're talking about," said Julie blankly.

"It's a man in slippers, and he comes toward you all slow and—and horrible!" Lex cried, shuddering.

Light dawned. Julie would have laughed, had it not been for this girl's deadly seriousness and her predicament. "Lex, that was Pushy!"

"Don't be silly, Pushy's a dog. I know when I hear one," said Lex icily.

"A St. Bernard shambling over bare wood sounds exactly like a man in carpet slippers," Julie explained. "He was coming to see who was in the kitchen. And you dropped the axe, and poor old Push cut himself."

"I didn't know that," said the girl. "The door was shut, and I heard this frightful noise, and I let go of my warning sign and it smashed. I can't imagine how you even knew what it was."

"Stash put it together, without telling Julie," said Monty. Things were coming into focus, but with blind spots here and there. "You left the outside door open, didn't you?"

"I don't remember. Probably."

"So Nana, who was in the kitchen, chased after you for a mile or two. But Pushy was shut in the rest of the house."

"*I* never let him out. I thought he was a ghost." She shivered again. "I was scared. I jumped in my car and took off down the back road at fifty. I didn't even see the beagle." Remembrance of her fright seemed to loosen her tongue. "I'd had your guided tour of the farm not very long before, when Dirk sweetly offered my services to help you school Cache," she said, shooting her brother a glare of pure rage. "I knew you fed at four o'clock, and that most hands would be busy with stabling horses from paddocks and feeding and doing up for the night. And I'd been in your house for a bottle of cola, and knew the layout. I just didn't know about the St. Bernard."

"So far," said the sheriff a little plaintively, "this is Greek to me."

"I'll fill you in later," said Monty. "How did Push get into the kitchen if you didn't open the inner door to see what was making the noise?"

"I wouldn't have opened that door for a million dollars," cried Alexis. "You people can laugh if you like, but there *are* ghosts, and I thought he was one!"

Julie thought, a girl who believed in ghosts that strongly would also believe that others could be frightened away by them. But a ghost that left you glass axes? That was really a little sick . . . of course, this poor girl *was* sick. "Next was the hounds getting loose," she said. "The afternoon I was here to feed them. You came back early, didn't you?"

"Yes, but I certainly never let any hounds loose! I drove up in the rain and heard you out back calling the beagle, so I took the van down to the stable. I walked back and saw you go inside, so I disconnected the battery wires of your car to stick you here, and went in the kitchen after awhile and prowled around till I saw you go into the study here. If you'd turned your head you'd have caught me. I went upstairs and dried off and lay down on my bed to think what I could do to really scare you, and I fell asleep."

"Same thing I did in this chair," nodded Julie.

"I slept for hours, and an awful bang wakened me."

"That was the door slamming in the wind. Then you let Pushy and Nana in."

"I did not!" the girl screeched at her, startling everyone. "I even made sure both doors were tight shut! And then I was going to start moaning and howling, only I—I was a little scared myself, it was so dark and the storm was fierce. And then I heard your ghost again. How could I guess it was a dog?" she demanded indignantly. "I was in that pitch-dark hall and here it was coming after me from the other end! I went out the front door and shut it and ran down to the stable. I waited there, and when the rain slacked off some, I went back and fixed your car so it would start, and I was going to come and scratch at the window but I was still frightened, so I just threw a rock in and ran to the barn again."

"I thought I saw you, but I wasn't sure," said Julie. "I mean, I didn't know it was you, it was just a dim figure."

"Well then, who let the hounds loose, and your dogs into the house? Tell *me* there aren't ghosts," said Lex with scorn.

"Could you try to get to the part about Sunbonnet?" the sheriff requested.

"Sorry, but she'd better take it in order," Monty said apologetically. "Some of us have been wondering for months about these things. I never knew about all this study business, though, except for Nana."

"Nana? What did she do?" Lex asked. She did not seem like a girl in trouble now; only like a girl engaged in a ferocious argument with a lot of imbeciles.

"She got her head stuck in a jar and banged around for ages. That would really have jolted you," Julie said, before she thought.

"It sure would have," Lex agreed. "Well, what do you want to know about next? I forget the order of all these things, I just did them as I thought of them."

"You moved the last fence of the gymnastic while Julie and I were tacking up," said Dirk quietly. Monty looked at him and could hardly imagine what terrible emotions were going on behind the stony, handsome face. "Didn't it occur to you that Julie could have been killed?" Dirk asked her.

"No. I wanted her shaken up and scared to come back. I moved the fence in and rubbed out the old marks where it had been sitting. Not everyone would have thought to do that," said Alexis proudly.

"No, that's right. Then you cut the stirrup leather of my saddle."

"And rubbed it and frayed it till it looked like anything but a cut, yes. And even that didn't stop you," she said venomously to Julie.

"And then, when Dirk gave you Morusan to bring me, you exchanged it for a blister."

"I knew you wouldn't know the difference. I hoped that when Cache was laid up, you'd take him home and stay away."

"To me, yes, I understand, sort of," said Julie, "but how could you do that to a horse?"

"He wasn't my horse."

"Holy old cow," said the sheriff quietly. Monty thought, My sentiments exactly. This was a girl whose whole life was bound up with animals. But then, it was even more so with her brother.

"And you frightened Dragonhold on the fox hunt, somehow," Julie said.

"Sure. It was easy. I tranked her with Rompin. You remember," Lex said, turning to Dirk eagerly. "I use it when I have to pull November Witch's mane, otherwise she's impossible! It only lasts twenty minutes or so." She looked at Julie again. "I just wanted you far enough behind the field so that I could hide On Target and get out the scarecrow. Did you see it? Did you see the face?"

"No. A scarecrow," said Julie, realizing that of course it had to have been that. The eeriness of the half-glimpsed figure came back to her. "With a white head."

"That's a bleach bottle! It has a great face painted on it, too. I'd taken it from its place and hidden it under that brush, and then the morning of the hunt it was ready to stick up at you as you took the jump. But I didn't have any luck," said Alexis, sagging back, "not once the whole time."

"Yes, you did," said Dirk. "You caused a great deal of pain, but you didn't do any real lasting damage. That's as lucky as you can get."

Alexis hung her head and at last began to cry. Her brother went on, inexorable. "So you tranquilized Dragon, and she couldn't keep pace with the field, and you dropped away yourself and laid in wait for her with a scarecrow, hoping that Julie would fall and hurt herself."

"Or be so petrified that she'd keep away!"

"But when that didn't work, you thought of stealing Bonnie."

"After a long time, yes. I thought up all sorts of neat things, but couldn't get any of them to jell. I even broke my alabaster owl. No, that was before. You sure don't scare easy," said the girl, still crying. "I figured Bonnie would do it, though, and it would have if you hadn't come right over here and found her so quick."

"How would I have connected that with Croydon?"

"I'd have studied out something."

The sheriff stood up. "In my opinion," he said gently, "you have a criminal case here, but nobody's going to want to pursue it. Right?" Julie and the two men nodded. "I'll just report the mare was found, then; I alerted the state police. But I'll want to be hearing further from you, Mr. Markham, on, ah, on what you decide to do about things."

"I'll call you shortly. And many thanks, Sam."

"It's okay, Dirk. Good luck."

"I soothed her with gumdrops," Lex said to no one in particular, as though seeking for a sign of approval of her cleverness. "Julie was always talking about Bonnie and her gumdrops."

"You're to go up and rest now, dear," said Dirk. "This has been a shock to you."

"All right, I guess I will." Alexis went to the door. "Are you going to keep visiting?" she asked Julie dully, and without waiting for an answer, left the room. They heard her go slowly upstairs.

Dirk looked at Julie and Monty hopelessly. "What can I say?"

"Nothing needs to be said," Monty gruffed, "except that I'm sorry, Dirk. I thought it was you all along. I even thought at one point that you might have been the boy who murdered the Croydons in this house, released from the asylum and come back . . . still out of your head. Nothing else made sense to me. I had no idea—"

"Neither did I, not until Nana bayed today and the whole terrible affair made sense to me. Because if Bonnie was here, it explained everything. Maybe I had suspicions before, especially after the ointment thing, but I sat on them and wouldn't recognize them." He sighed. "No, Monty, I wasn't the Croydon boy. He's still locked up. But for years he's claimed that he's sane; that he *had* gone out of his mind, yes, but only after he walked into this room and found his foster parents butchered. He recovered his memory a few years later, after shock therapy actually, but of course nobody believed him. Except me."

"You, Dirk?"

"That's one reason I bought Croydon, though I'd have done it anyway, I think, for Lex and the horses and dogs. . . ."

"Who are you?" Julie asked, for there was suddenly more mystery here than before.

"I'm the kid who met Carl Croydon that night to go to the movies. We were pals, both orphans, you know, me for a few months, Carl a long time back and adopted, but still an orphan. I never believed that he was guilty. He could be a little wild sometimes, as weren't most of us? But he didn't have it in him, sane or crazy, to kill anything. I *knew* that boy. I knew that he'd simply lost his grip on reality when the two people he loved best were murdered. I'm still sure of it, but I haven't found anything to prove it." He stopped, and gave a strangled sound like a dying man. "I knew that boy. Did you hear me say that? *I knew my sister.* And she might have killed Julie, three or four times. Maybe I've been wrong about Carl all this time, too."

"But I think we can prove that now, one way or the

other," said Julie. She walked to the hearthstone and pulled back the rug that now lay beside it. She tugged at the board and got it up. The axe still rested in its hiding place, and beside it an empty metal cashbox. They all bent over the cavity.

"Don't touch it!" shouted Dirk. "Look at that crusted blood—there are fingerprints all over it! Preserved all these years—he must have gone around carrying the thing until the blood was drying—Monty, for the love of heaven, stop the sheriff before he's gone!"

Monty was off out of the room. Julie and Dirk stared at each other across the hole in the floor. "I've said it before," he told her in a kind of awed whisper, "you're the best piece of luck I ever ran into in my life. How'd you find it?"

"Snooping around," she said frankly.

They straightened up. "Can you forgive Lex, Julie? I know you have a terrific capacity for forgiveness, but . . ."

"You don't carry grudges against people who are sick, do you?" she said uncomfortably.

Then the room was full of deputies and the sheriff and everyone was talking at once, and Julie even forgot for a few minutes that her great and gallant mare Sunbonnet had been rescued.

Chapter 16

Although a number of mysterious incidents remained to be cleared up, and everyone was curious about both Alexis and the old Croydon House enigma, no one felt quite right about calling Dirk for a few days; so that when he phoned to ask if they'd come and bring Stash or Leon over to see a horse of his that had an ailment the vet couldn't even identify, it was a relief. Julie and Monty piled in the car with Leon, Stash, Pushy, and Nana (who was on a leash), and they drove to Croydon Farm.

Dirk was rather drawn-looking, but smiled his old natural grin as he greeted them. "Come look at the horse first—it's Castle Creek, Lex's show jumper, and I can't make out what's ailing him."

"What are the symptoms?" asked Leon, and their path to the stable was strewn with technical terms and bemused hypotheses. He and Stash examined the gelding thoroughly.

"Shoo, no problem," said Stash. "You take some lily leaves—"

"Stash Watkins, get out of that prehistoric swamp!" said Leon. "There's medicines aplenty will fix that fellow without your blame lily leaves! Dirk, you send for some—"

"Won't do any good," said Stash, shaking his head sadly. "No goop in a bottle's gonna do it, Dirk. Lily leaves wrapped around—"

"I hope I never get as old and set in my ways as you, you codger! Dirk, three good doses of—"

"You got as old as me twenty years ago! Dirk, it's lily leaves that'll fix that boy up, and nothing else."

"Whoa! I'll try both," laughed Dirk. "Let's go up for

167

some coffee, and I'll write them down. What's a lily leaf, Stash?"

"Something the witch doctors use in Ohio," said Leon.

In the study once more, they all sat on the edges of their chairs until Dirk had brought coffee and rolls. Then Julie asked it. "How's Alexis?"

"I can talk frankly to all of you, because you know everything that she did," said Dirk, standing by the fireplace and looking at them in turn. "She's been examined by an excellent psychiatrist, who prescribes a long course of intensive treatment to bring her out of the fantasy world she's lived in, and give her a sense of values that— I'm ashamed to admit I never realized—she sadly lacks. She'll be away quite a while."

"Can I say goodbye to her?" asked Julie.

"She's gone."

"Oh, I am sorry! Maybe I can visit her?"

"In a while, I think it would help. There were moments, before she left, when it seemed to strike her that she'd been as unfair to you as a person could be, and there must be a streak of guilt a yard wide about that, somewhere inside of her. Now," he said, shaking the unhappy topic away, "about Carl Croydon."

"He didn't do it," said Leon suddenly.

"He did not. He's vindicated completely. The axe did yield fingerprints—those of a convicted maniac, who's long since dead. He was never suspected even after they caught him, because Carl's 'confession' had closed the Croydon case. So young Croydon—young thirty-year-old Croydon—is being released this week, having been certified sane. I'll try to, well, help him put his life together once more, although I'm certain he won't want to return to this place, not ever."

"Dirk," said Stash, "could I ask you something? How come I never could get a line on you? I did some investigatin' back when we all sort of wondered about you, but nobody ever connected you with the Croydon boy, and Monty tells me you were the one persuaded him to go to the law."

"They kept my name out of the papers. Part of it was just common decency, because I was a kid, and part was old Sam's doing—the sheriff, you know. He said publicity of that kind wouldn't do me any good. He helped later, too, when I wanted to keep in touch with Carl."

"I couldn't even find out if Carl Croydon was alive or dead."

"Not many people know. Everyone will soon. I hope they'll be sensible and kind about it when he turns up in Meriden."

"Good folks around here," said Leon positively. "They'll treat him right. How is he with horses?"

"I don't know whether he ever saw one up close."

"Bring him over to Fieldstone, might be we could find some kind of rough work for him if he'd like." Leon shook his head. "I recollect his folks so well. Like to help their boy."

Dirk smiled. "It's a promise. Of course, for all I know he may want to be a writer, or a cobbler, or some other wild profession that hasn't anything to do with horses."

"Nope," said Leon, "you just said he was certified sane!"

"The cashbox," said Monty, "was that the reason for the murders, do you know?"

"I'd guess it was. The killer probably got them to confess where their little bit of household money was hidden, and then decided the axe could go in there too. Strange," Dirk said, "it happened in this room, when I was seventeen, and condemned a friend to more than a dozen years of lost life, and now I don't even feel odd here."

"That's because it's all over, and the ghosts, who weren't here anyway, are really laid to rest," said Julie.

"Funny, that's what Lex said. Except that she thought they *had* been here." He set down his cup. "Listen, before you all go, can I show you my new benches down at the kennel? It's an idea I got from a transplanted Englishman at the meet."

"Sure, sure thing," said everyone. They trooped out, Julie retrieving Nana from the hitching post to which she'd thoughtfully been tied, and calling to Pushy, they walked to the kennels.

"I don't see any benches," said the girl, who was walking arm-in-arm with Monty in a rather self-conscious manner.

"In the lodging room, silly girl!"

"What's *that?*"

"The building where they sleep, of course. Come around the fence, we'll look in through the other door." They did so. "See, the wooden sleeping platforms covered with wheat straw? Those are 'benches' and they're a lot better for the pups than sleeping on mats and blankets on the floor. The wheat keeps their coats clean, and the raised benches prevent any possibility of drafts or dampness. Neat?"

"You are so good to your animals," said Julie. "You're a good man, Dirk."

"Thanks. It remains to be seen," said he, eyeing Monty, "whether I'm the better man, or wind up as just the best man."

"That's too deep for me," said Julie, who understood him perfectly.

"A man can only try his best," said Monty, and chuckled, which he could not have managed to do several days before. "But you don't have the field to yourself by any means."

"I've lately become aware of that," said Dirk.

They began to walk slowly back to the house and their car. Leon said to Stash, "I didn't hear you say *uh-oh!*"

"I don't need to say *uh-oh,* because Monty has finally got the bit in his teeth, as non-racing folks say, and he may be a late starter but he's gonna be a whirlwind from the far turn on down to the finish line." said Stash.

"I'm inclined to agree with you, father."

"That's good thinking, pappy."

"Hey, what's Pushy doing?" said Julie suddenly, turning to look for her St. Bernard. "Push!"

The huge dog was standing beside the door of the hounds' kennel and pawing at the white knob. As they watched, he got his great foot wrapped around it and bore down. The knob turned, he let go, and the door swung slowly open.

"Oh, what a clever trick!" Julie shouted. "When did you—oh!"

"When did he, indeed. He did quite a while ago," said Monty.

The hounds began to pour forth, and Dirk shouted at them, but in vain. They were eager to romp freely, to swirl round and round the humans, to give tongue and put their forefeet on people's chests and all sorts of forbidden things. They were off duty, after all, and they knew it.

"That's how he got into the kitchen of my cottage! That's how *he* let the hounds out that other night, the rascal! And that's how come he and Nana were in Croydon and scared me half to fits!"

"He's always been a pusher, hence his name," said Monty to Dirk. "But now he's a turner, too."

"Pushy W. Turner. A fine-sounding name," Dirk said.

"Well, that solves the final question, and the biggest mystery of all," said Leon to Julie.

"What's that?"

"Why, the very first thing that happened that we couldn't explain! How Nana got out of the kitchen and ate up your priceless quilt! Pushy opened the door for her."

"Oh, my gosh," said Julie.

"Dirk," said Monty, as the hounds' din drowned out all speech at a distance of over two feet, "I'm at the track a lot, and pretty soon Julie's going to be totally occupied with bringing Bonnie back into racing condition; but I know you're going to be lonely here with Lex away . . ."

"I certainly am," said Dirk.

"Well, don't forget you have plenty of friends at Fieldstone," said Monty gruffly, and held out his hand.

Dirk shook it hard. "You almost make me say that I'll withdraw from any competition with you, Monty."

"No good man ought to do that till the results go up on the board," said Monty.

They grinned at each other, as Julie embraced clever

Pushy and told him not to do it again, and Nana tugged
at her leash because she smelled a rabbit, and Stash and
Leon winked at each other, and the foxhounds swirled
around in belling, bugling chaos.

More SIGNET Young Adult Titles You'll Enjoy

- [ ] **DELPHA GREEN AND COMPANY by Vera and Bill Cleaver.** (#Y6907—$1.25)

- [ ] **THE WHYS AND WHEREFORES OF LITTABELLE LEE by Vera and Bill Cleaver.** (#Y7225—$1.25)

- [ ] **ELLEN GRAE AND LADY ELLEN GRAE by Vera and Bill Cleaver.** (#W8689—$1.50)

- [ ] **GROVER by Vera and Bill Cleaver.** (#Y6714—$1.25)

- [ ] **I WOULD RATHER BE A TURNIP by Vera and Bill Cleaver.** (#Y7034—$1.25)

- [ ] **ME TOO by Vera and Bill Cleaver.** (#Y6519—$1.25)

- [ ] **THE MOCK REVOLT by Vera and Bill Cleaver.** (#Y7502—$1.25)

- [ ] **WHERE THE LILIES BLOOM by Vera and Bill Cleaver.** (#W8065—$1.50)

- [ ] **MATTY DOOLIN by Catherine Cookson.** (#Y7126—$1.25)*

- [ ] **SONG OF THE SHAGGY CANARY by Phyllis Anderson Wood.** (#Y7859—$1.25)

- [ ] **YOUR BIRD IS HERE, TOM THOMPSON by Phyllis Anderson Wood.** (#Y8192—$1.25)

- [ ] **I THINK THIS IS WHERE I CAME IN by Phyllis Anderson Wood.** (#Y7753—$1.25)

- [ ] **I'VE MISSED A SUNSET OR THREE by Phyllis Anderson Wood.** (#Y7944—$1.25)

* Not available in Canada

Buy them at your local

bookstore or use coupon

on next page for ordering.